CROAK AND DAGGER

A WILDWOOD WITCH MYSTERY: BOOK 4

ELLE ADAMS

To be notified when Elle Adams's next book is released, sign up to her author newsletter.

1

If anyone had told me that the trickiest part of being Head Witch would be flying on a broomstick while carrying a sceptre, I'd have been sceptical to say the least. Yet the weight of the long, pointed stick made my flight path lopsided, and steering one-handed meant that if anyone hit me with a spell from behind, I'd be in for a humiliating tumble to the ground.

Luckily, nobody was foolish enough to sneak up on the Head Witch *and* the leader of the Wildwood Coven at the same time, let alone above the expanse of the Wildwood itself. As our broomsticks touched down on the hillside, my squirrel familiar, Tansy, leapt onto the grass and launched into a joyful sprint towards the forest. Mum and Ramsey followed, along with their own familiars—Horace the orange-and-white cat and Prickles the hedgehog—at a more sedate pace. As for me, my brief rush of relief at seeing the cluster of houses that comprised Wildwood Heath was immediately followed by surprise that I'd felt any relief at all.

I'd never in my life thought I'd be relieved, even glad, to see my childhood home, but my reaction said volumes about how my life had turned on its head in recent weeks.

"See?" I gestured at the rooftops visible through the trees ahead of us. "Nothing's caught on fire while we were gone. It's all fine."

"We have less than a day to prepare for our guests' arrival," Mum reprimanded me. "It's not *fine*, Robin. If we're not careful, the guests will show up without us having adequate time to prepare."

"You spent weeks arranging everything *before* we left," I pointed out. "As well as preparing for a dozen other impossible scenarios."

From the way Mum had reacted to our departure, you'd think we'd been embarking on a year-long round trip to the moon, not a week-long holiday a couple of hours away in the south of England. Admittedly, we'd returned several days later than planned due to a side quest of sorts on our way home in the form of a baby dragon who'd been separated from its parents, but as far as I was concerned, that was a valid enough reason to deviate from the planned schedule. At the time, Mum and Ramsey had agreed, but their agitation had grown in the past day, and I could understand why they'd become concerned about how the town had fared in our absence.

"I had to," Mum said. "With the coven leader *and* the head of the police out of town at the same time, the chances were high that someone would seize the opportunity to make trouble."

I glanced at my brother, whose usually impeccable blond hair was windswept from his flight and who wore jeans and a jacket that were utterly unlike the neat uniform he wore ninety-nine percent of the time. "You didn't both have to come, I told you."

"Ramsey needed the holiday more than you did."

She wasn't wrong, but the notion that I could have ever persuaded my notoriously workaholic brother to take a single day off was laughable. "He volunteered. As did you."

As the head of Wildwood Heath's police force, Ramsey had been in dire need of a break after a draining murder investigation had taken over the police's resources for a week, and Mum had flat-out refused to stay behind. As a result, we'd set off on a family holiday for the first time since Ramsey and I had been kids. Frankly, the real miracle was that we'd lasted a full week in each other's company without someone ending up cursed.

"I did," Ramsey said stiffly. "But we're home now, and it's time to put the past week behind us. We have work to do."

No surprise that he'd want to get back to his routine as swiftly as possible. He and Mum had come up with so many contingency plans before we'd left that I'd started to worry we *would* return to find the town on fire, but the forests surrounding the small village of Wildwood Heath were as pristine as ever. Tansy scampered around, chasing birds and the local grey squirrels—it was a point of pride that she was the only red squirrel in the region—and generally reminding everyone who was boss.

I, however, felt my good mood deflating with every step I took. The past week had been the most fun I'd had since before my return to Wildwood Heath had put sceptre-shaped handcuffs around my wrists, and it was completely worth the panic of coming back and realising that we had less than a day to prepare for the other four Head Witches of the Midlands to arrive.

As we made our way down the winding path through the woodland, Mum's manner grew more agitated.

"The others are due to arrive tomorrow afternoon, but I expect at least one of them will show up early," she said. "Isadora and Acacia have a habit of trying to outdo one another."

"See, that's where we differ," I said. "I'd say the person who arrives last is the real winner, because they got to waste less time waiting for everyone else."

Mum gave me a sideways look. "You'll be doing more than just waiting, Robin. It won't be a regular day at the office."

"I was never under the impression that it would be." The location of each meeting of the Head Witches varied, but the coven had collectively agreed it was better to choose a familiar setting for my first major council meeting. Five Head Witches would attend, including me, and Mum was the one who'd taken it upon herself to arrange the accommodations for our guests, since she was the head of the Wildwood Coven and therefore their host, despite my holding the title of Head Witch.

At one time, both titles had belonged to my grandmother, but her untimely death a few weeks prior had seen a mad scramble to find a replacement. Unlike the title of coven leader, which went to a vote, the Head Witch was chosen directly by the magical sceptre she wielded. I still had no idea why the sceptre had picked me out of all the other available options, considering Mum was the one with the contacts and the years of experience in helping to run a coven. I was the family screwup who'd struck out alone and had barely any experience to speak of, but the sceptre's word was law, and so we'd prepared the best we could.

In the end, there was nothing to worry about except not making a fool of myself in front of all the distinguished magical representatives of the region. No pressure.

"You've already met Jemima," Mum said. "That ought to help with the adjustment."

True. That had been one reason for our trip—so I could meet at least one other Head Witch in a slightly less intimidating environment—but the short time I'd had to prepare for this first summit didn't feel like enough.

Granted, Mum had pointed out that most Head Witches learned through experience, and being an unconventional Head Witch didn't mean that I couldn't do the same. Her comment was supposed to be a compliment on how well I'd adapted to the unexpected role thrust upon my head, but my life for the next few months would consist of meeting after tedious meeting, and the real challenge would be pretending to give a crap about coven budgets and other joyless drama that I'd wanted no part in. Fun times.

All too soon, we reached the end of the path which led to the enclave where the leading members of our coven lived. As our group approached my childhood home, movement stirred behind the curtains of the house next to ours, as if someone had their eye on our return. I had no doubt that Aunt Shannon was eagerly waiting to find out if we'd learned why the sceptre had picked me as Head Witch and not her, but that question remained unanswered despite our visit to a magical library that contained resources beyond most other places in the paranormal world. I'd read countless accounts of past Head Witches and the challenges they'd faced, but none of those, to my knowledge, would rather play *Pokémon Go* than sit through a meeting on coven budgeting woes.

There was a first time for everything, I supposed.

Mum cast an unreadable look at her sister's house before unlocking the door to her own. Meanwhile, I pointed my wand at my suitcase, transporting it up to my room to unpack later. "I'm heading out for a bit."

Mum paused with one hand on the doorframe. "Yes, you should get your office ready for tomorrow. Good idea."

"I'm not going to the office now," I said flatly. "I won't drag poor Chloe back to work on a weekend. She can wait until tomorrow morning."

"And what is your priority, exactly?" Mum rotated on her heel, eyes narrowing at me. "Seeing that... Harvey Walton?"

"Seeing my dad," I corrected, though I had every intention of meeting up with Harvey later. Mentioning my dad shut down Mum's questions though, which was the plan.

Her expression blanked out. "Of course. Don't get back too late, will you?"

Mum continued into the house, followed by her familiar, while Tansy scampered up to sit on my shoulder. My parents' split had been amicable enough, though Dad had drawn the short straw as usual thanks to the local tabloid press's habit of gleefully reporting on every streak of misfortune that fell upon my family. Dad seemed much happier away from the spotlight with his new partner, Jessica, who had two kids of her own. Mum claimed not to envy him his newly stress-free life, but she kept her interactions with him to a minimum. As for Ramsey, I was still waiting for my brother to get over his stubbornness and initiate contact with Dad again. For a brief moment, I wondered if our recent holiday might have softened him up a little, but when I cast him a hopeful glance, he averted his gaze and went into the house. Ah well. It was worth a shot.

Tansy and I headed down the woodland trail towards the cottage where Dad lived with his wife and her two werewolf kids from her previous marriage, Jake and Spike. This would be my last chance to visit him before our guests showed up, and while I hoped to meet up with Harvey later that evening, giving my friends an update on my holiday would have to wait. Granted, I might be able to sneak in a visit to Rowan at lunchtime tomorrow, since she worked full-time at the werewolf-run cafe, Were's My Coffee?, and even my mother wouldn't deny me the chance to get a last caffeine fix before the other Head Witches arrived.

Rowan's new job was the reason she hadn't been able to come on our trip. She had to pay all her own bills since she'd left her family's home, and while I was glad she'd been able to get away from Aunt Shannon's influence, it would have been nice to have someone to back me up during the many arguments I'd had with my mum and brother over the past week. When they teamed up against me, it was like trying to break down a wall with my bare hands.

Of course, I always had Tansy. Her fluffy tail flickered in and out of sight as she chased blackbirds out of trees while I walked down the woodland path which curved around the northern side of town, savouring the peacefulness of the moment. I had an inkling such interludes would be in short supply over the next week.

Upon reaching the neat cottage where my dad lived, I rapped on the door. He answered a moment later, a wide smile on his round face.

"Hey, Robin." Dad wrapped me in a hug. "How was your trip?"

"Eventful." That was a mild way of putting it, really. "Tansy, want to go outside and play with the kids? I bet they'll be happy to see you."

Tansy had already lived through the mayhem of the past week once, so she amused herself playing with the two werewolf kids outside, supervised by Jessica, while I gave Dad the rundown.

"I'm glad you were able to get away for a bit, at least," Dad said when I'd finished. "Back to work tomorrow, right?"

"Yeah, and the other Head Witches are arriving in the afternoon."

"Right, that's it," said Dad. "Nervous?"

"A little, but I know what to expect."

My phone buzzed with a text message from Harvey, and a smile came to my mouth. He and I had messaged frequently over the past week—mostly him updating me on what I was missing at home while I vented about my family—and as I'd hoped, he was free that evening to meet me at the Fox's Den, the local pub.

"Who's that?" asked Dad. "New boyfriend, right?"

"Yep." The thought brought me out in happy tingles since our relationship was shiny and new and fresh out of the box. It was the sole pleasant surprise in a sea of upheavals since my return to Wildwood Heath, and our week apart had only heightened the anticipation of seeing him again.

"Go on," said Dad. "You want to go and meet him now, right?"

"Yeah… this is going to be my last night off for a while," I acknowledged. "It's been great seeing you again though. I'll drop by for a longer visit when our esteemed guests have left."

I went outside to pick up Tansy and say hi to Jessica and the kids before leaving the cottage and heading back down the woodland path. Since I was still wearing the clothes I'd flown home in, I wanted to change before my date with Harvey, though I'd rather have avoided the inevitable conversation with my family about my choice in romantic partners.

Unlike the other members of my close family, Dad didn't judge me for wanting to date someone ordinary and would accept me no matter what choices I made. Mum and Ramsey were trickier, though we'd reached a compromise: Mum had agreed to stay out of my romantic life on the condition that I did my job as Head Witch without fail. Yet another reason I had to get through this week without any major screwups.

Mum reacted to news of my plans for the evening with the usual long-suffering look, but she didn't argue, so I went upstairs to change into a fresh outfit before heading for the Fox's Den. The shifter-owned pub was one of my favourite places in town. Possibly for that reason, my family members were not fans of the place, but we'd agreed that they wouldn't attempt to control what I did in my free time as long as I complied with the demands of being Head Witch. So far, it was working out well.

I picked out a worn wooden table near the window to wait for Harvey and ordered both of us our favourite drinks. Not long after, he entered the pub. Tall, broad, and as handsome with his feet on the ground as he was in the sky, Harvey had been the one unexpected perk of my return to Wildwood Heath. Of course, the fact that he'd known me before the Head Witch title had been affixed to my head didn't hurt either.

Harvey smiled at me. "Hey, Robin."

"Hey." I greeted him with a kiss—brief since we were in public—and sat down at the table. "I managed to wrangle the evening off, but it's back to the usual tomorrow."

"So, how was your trip?" he asked. "Relaxing?"

"Try 'hectic,'" I said. "My family doesn't know *how* to relax, but even if they did, this was never just a holiday. You heard most of it already when I messaged you."

"Yes, but I've missed hearing your voice."

I grinned. "Then I'll oblige. Which part did you want to hear about? The bit when we got lost in the middle of nowhere and I had to ask a pigeon for directions, or when my mother decided to reprimand the owner of the library, who was nice enough to let us borrow their books, for supposed breaches of magical law?"

His brows rose. "Never a dull moment, is there?"

"No, and a refreshing lack of hours sitting at a desk." Too bad my family hadn't appreciated it as much as I had and had tried to strong-arm me into staying indoors to read the library's accounts of past Head Witches instead of enjoying the nice weather. Needless to say, Tansy and I hadn't been keen on the idea.

"I'm glad you got a break for a bit," he said. "You met one Head Witch already though?"

"Yeah, Jemima. She was… fine." Jemima's bright clothing and jewels were far from the image in my mind of stuffy witches who were stuck several decades in the past, but she was in her fifties and still closer to my age than most of the others I'd meet at the summit. "The others are arriving tomorrow."

"That soon? You barely got back."

"Thanks to our detour. The baby dragon incident threw off our schedule, and now Mum is acting as if the town has turned upside-down in her absence. Never mind that she left everyone with in-depth instructions for the entire week, including what to do in the event of a hundred possible emergency scenarios."

"I can imagine," he responded. "It's what she's like. She has to be in control."

"That's one reason I can't say I'm looking forwards to this visit," I admitted. "The other Head Witches will expect *me* to be in control, and I have to act like I am, no matter what Mum tries to do. If I don't, they'll think the town is weak and that the Head Witch is under her mother's thumb."

"That sounds like more her problem than yours."

"You aren't wrong, but I don't need any more complications than I already have." I absently stirred my drink with my straw. "I'm supposed to be more worried someone will send assassins after me. Or worse, the press."

The latter were a fair possibility, since they'd been waiting on tenterhooks for me to make a public fool of myself ever since I'd taken the title of Head Witch, and the meeting might be the opportune moment for them to slither into my life again. The local tabloids had been a nuisance throughout my childhood, badgering my family and printing outlandish stories about us, but I'd beaten them twice over in the past weeks—first through kicking them out of town after they'd crossed too many lines while reporting on my grandmother's funeral and secondly by ensuring my first meeting with a fellow Head Witch was low-key and off the grid. That way, any unintentional breaches of etiquette I made wouldn't end up being headline news.

"They should have more sense than to come back," Harvey said. "I expect they'll be sniffing around for news, but they aren't worth wasting time with."

"Gotta save all my attention for the potential assassins." I sipped my drink. "Nah, I'm not too worried about the press. If they can't get in, they'll make up some story about me scandalising everyone by not knowing the right way to open a door."

He arched a brow. "Is that likely to be a concern?"

"Not to anyone who's worth bothering with." I shrugged one shoulder, trying to find words to convey my general unease with the situation. "No... it's more the assumptions that bug me, but I can't do anything about those."

It was no secret that I'd walked away from Wildwood Heath as soon as I'd been old enough to leave, and I wasn't used to being tied down to anything—not a place, a person, or a title. Yes, I'd had to move back in with my family a few times when I'd been between jobs, but that had been temporary. It was hard out there for a witch trying to make it alone, but I hadn't wanted to fall back on my family's offer of a job within the coven and resign myself to being trapped in my childhood home for the rest of my life.

Now? The universe had conspired to take that choice away, and with the title of Head Witch resting uncomfortably on my head, I was trapped for the foreseeable future. To an outsider though, it looked more as if I'd finally grown up and seen the sense in being the person my family wanted me to be rather than making decisions for my own sake. Nothing could have been further from the truth.

"It'll be fine," he reassured me. "There have been all kinds of Head Witches. There's no textbook definition."

"Not all of them have *stayed* Head Witch though. Some met unpleasant ends or quit or…" I trailed off before I made my own nerves worse than they already were. "Granted, a kid got chosen as Head Witch the other month up north, so it could be far worse."

"Exactly." He reached out for my hand. "I'm here for you if you need to vent in the meantime. I know exactly nothing about being Head Witch, so I won't judge you for anything."

"That helps." It did too. The number of people not watching my every move was in short supply, after all, and while not everything was within my control, a lot was riding on this meeting.

Still, as long as I stuck to the plan, everything ought to go smoothly. I hoped.

2

Bright and early the following morning, I found myself facing my first Head Witch of the day. Or should that be *former* Head Witch? My grandmother's ghost hovered next to the desk in the office that had once been hers, her expression disapproving as she surveyed the room. "Look at this mess."

"Don't blame me. I wasn't even here." Yes, there were stacks of paperwork everywhere, but they'd seemingly materialised of their own accord. Chloe had been off all week—I'd insisted she take a holiday too—so Mum must have come to the office early and dropped off a week's worth of reports. How generous of her.

"You left the responsibility behind, and now look at what happened." Grandma's ghost gave a sweeping gesture that sent several papers flying into the air.

"Whoa." I grabbed the papers before they fluttered to the ground. She hadn't been able to do that beforehand, but I'd bet she'd spent the past week practising using her

14

poltergeist abilities out of boredom. "I'd have thought you'd be happy to have the office to yourself for a bit."

My grandmother complained when I so much as moved a piece of paper, so I'd thought my absence would be like a holiday to her. Or a chance to pretend she was still Head Witch. I could just picture her swooping around the office, giving orders to invisible servants.

"The sceptre wasn't here." Grandma pursed her lips. "The office isn't the same without it."

Ah. She'd missed the sceptre. Probably more than she missed me, though I couldn't entirely fault her for that, since she'd carried the sceptre for decades and had only been parted from it upon her death. Still, she was hardly oblivious to the fact that the sceptre and I were stuck together by tradition and not by choice.

"Relax. I took good care of it." I gestured at the side of the desk, where the long instrument stood propped up against the wooden edge. That was a point of annoyance to Grandma, too, who was of the opinion that I ought to store the sceptre in its protective glass case whenever I was in the office. Considering I'd faced at least one murder attempt inside this very room, I was content to ignore her opinion on that one.

"She did." My assistant, Chloe, briefly glanced up from her desk on the other side of the room, typing away at her laptop as if she'd never been absent. "Also, I'm the one who brought in the paperwork."

"Ignore her," I told Chloe. "She's had nobody to complain to all week, so she has to make up for lost time."

Grandma scoffed and drifted past my assistant's desk, where her familiar, Carmilla, lay sleeping on top of yet another stack of paperwork. I could say with certainty that she, for one, hadn't missed me being around. "If you ask me, you don't need to take the sceptre with you whenever you go on one of your excursions. It's a valuable artefact, not a toy."

Good lord. "I'm aware of that. You do know I have to spend the next few months travelling all over the country to meet the other Head Witches, don't you? It's kind of a necessary part of the job."

"*I'm* aware of that." Grandma mimicked my voice. "This latest trip of yours wasn't part of your job. It was a holiday."

"To research the sceptre and try to find out why it chose me as its wielder," I corrected. "If you have a problem, take it up with my mother. It was her idea."

I should have guessed our sudden departure would have annoyed her. As a ghost, my grandmother was bound to this part of town—or possibly to the coven's headquarters alone—and was therefore unable to follow me away from Wildwood Heath. I couldn't deny I was glad for that limitation. The rest of my family members and their familiars showing up in unexpected places to reprimand me was quite enough on its own, thanks.

Grandma sniffed in answer. "I think my daughter has enough to worry about, don't you?"

And I don't? Honestly, I was pretty sure Grandma hadn't been this much of a complainer back when she was Head Witch, but as a ghost, she had the freedom to act in a manner that she'd never been able to get away with in life. Not just because fewer people could actually see her but because she just plain didn't give a crap anymore.

As for the former, she was only visible to those of us who could see ghosts, but since most of the witches in my coven had that talent, I didn't usually give it much thought. That might not be true of the other Head Witches, however, since a third of all witches had that ability. It wasn't a prerequisite of the position by any means, but I did wonder if it'd occurred to the others that my predecessor might have stuck around after her untimely death.

"Do you want me to tell the other Head Witches you exist?" I queried. "Or save it for an emergency?"

"No."

I blinked. "No to both options? What do you want me to do then?"

"Tell nobody I'm here," she said firmly. "I've more than earned the right to retire in peace."

She wasn't wrong, but before I could formulate a reply, the door opened, and Mum came into the office. "Ready?"

"What, six hours early?" I raised a brow. "I'm ready for the Head Witches, but unless I want them to be buried alive in paperwork, then I have to clear some of this off my desk."

"They won't be coming into your office, Robin."

"Certainly not," Grandma said. "I won't have them nosing around in here."

I gave her an eye roll. "She claims she doesn't want anyone to know she exists."

Mum drew in a breath. "Yes, I think that's wise."

"Uh… why?" I hadn't exactly planned to rely on my predecessor as a source of advice while the others were here, but I also hadn't expected Mum to so readily support Grandma's decision to hide out of sight.

Mum levelled me with a stare. "Among the Head Witches, knowledge is power."

"Well, that's me screwed then." I spoke in a light tone, though a not-insignificant part of me was genuinely worried that my shallow pool of knowledge and experience would doom me from the outset.

"You read all the records we got from the library, didn't you?"

"Yes, I did." The accounts written by former Head Witches had shown they almost all experienced doubts about their capabilities, but none of them had been in a situation quite like mine. Mum had insisted on me putting my new camera to use by photographing each page from the book to consult later if I needed to, but I couldn't exactly bring them to the meeting with the other Head Witches. "They don't say anything about whether it's wise to lie to the other Head Witches' faces if one of them asks if my predecessor stuck around."

"I doubt it'll occur to any of them," Mum said. "In any case, I've told them to land outside in the road, not on the hillside. That ought to stop any reporters from tailing them into the town."

"Good call." While I'd kicked the press out of town weeks ago, they might well be lying in wait to ambush the other Head Witches upon their arrival and would sneak back in the instant I let down my guard. "Hope the others have more sense than to give them the time of day."

"If they show up early, we need a game plan," she went on. "I've planned a tour of the town for them. Chloe, take a look at that when you have a moment."

"Mum, leave her be," I said. "We're trying to prepare for the meeting, and it's a bit difficult with you throwing more tasks at us."

Mum didn't take the hint. Throughout the morning,

she kept ducking in and out of my office to ask questions and repeat advice she'd already given me a dozen times. She had more on her plate than I did, since she'd taken it upon herself to arrange our visitors' accommodation and catering, but that left her with plenty of time to drop in on me with her colour-coded schedule in hand and insist that I check every detail.

"This is unnecessary," I protested.

"No, it isn't." She shoved the paper under my nose. "Look it over."

I think someone's nervous. The trouble was, her nerves made mine worse, which came with unintended side effects. When a pigeon crashed into the window, drawn by the waves of agitation radiating from my nerves, I put my foot down.

"Unless you want a storm of feathers and bird droppings to greet the other Head Witches, you're going to have to tone it down." I pushed the schedule back into Mum's hand. "You've already told me the times, names, dates, and goddess only knows what else a thousand times. If anything, I'm more likely to get them mixed up than I was before."

Mum began to speak, and then the schedule fell from her hand as the sound of sweeping broomsticks descending came from outside.

My heart dropped. "That can't be them. Not this early."

"Yes, it can." Mum fled the office so quickly that she might as well have conjured up a broom of her own, while Grandma's ghost drifted to the back corner as if to hide herself behind the filing cabinets.

My wide eyes met Chloe's, and she rose to her feet as well. "We'll be fine. You're ready."

I gave a shaky nod. "Right."

Hoping the Head Witches hadn't flown into the swarm of birds I'd inadvertently drawn into town, I grabbed the sceptre and hurried out of the office. My heart drummed in anticipation as I crossed the lobby to the front door, where a group of cloaked individuals had landed in the road outside the coven's headquarters.

As I pushed open the door, they waved their wands, and their broomsticks and suitcases vanished, presumably to their place of accommodation. I didn't recognise anyone among the arrivals except for Jemima, who I'd already met. She wore a sky-blue coat patterned with stars, and her silver hair had been enhanced with magic so that it sparkled.

She extended a hand bedecked in rings towards me. "It's a pleasure to meet you again, Head Witch."

"You too." When Mum cast me a sideways look, I put on a more formal tone. "Pleasure to meet you, too, Head Witch."

"Looks like I'm the first here," Jemima commented.

I looked at her cloaked companions. "Wait, these aren't the other Head Witches?"

"No, they're my fellow coven members."

A flush crept up my cheeks at the mistake. "Ah, okay."

Mum cleared her throat. "The others aren't far behind."

I lifted my head, seeing another flock of witches riding broomsticks towards us. As we watched, they flew into a formation and waved their wands, conjuring letters formed of sparks that spelled out "Head Witch Mavis Willow." They descended in a flash of brightness, which coalesced around the central figure in their group and the sceptre in her hand.

Despite the pomp and circumstance, the grey-haired witch who carried the sceptre looked almost ordinary when the brightness had faded. Her deep-green cloak flared behind her as she stepped off her broomstick and held out a hand. "I am Mavis Willow. Pleasure to meet you."

"Robin Wildwood. Same to you." When we shook hands, I noticed her palms were calloused as if she spent a lot of time outdoors. A green toad perched on her shoulder. Her familiar, I assumed, an unusual choice among Head Witches. Not that I was one to talk, because my own familiar was currently chasing pigeons around the coven's garden without having noticed the newcomers' arrival.

While Mavis greeted Jemima, more broomsticks descended. Everyone must have been determined to be the first to arrive, like Mum had said, so her endless fussing hadn't been entirely wasted after all.

A thin, wispy-looking woman stepped off the next broom, her sceptre thicker than her arm. Eyeing me with marked disdain, she reached out a claw-like hand. "I am Acacia Bracken." When she shook my hand, her grip was surprisingly strong. "And you must be Robin Wildwood."

"That's me... ah, pleasure to meet you," I added when Mum gave me a sideways look warning me to play my part.

At that moment, there came a flurry of noise that sounded like cannon fire mixed with fireworks. Every nearby bird took flight in alarm, and the flock of broomsticks that followed was all bright gold. Their riders, however, wore dull colours—with one exception. The

Head Witch, dressed in gold robes to match her broom-stick, glided elegantly to a stop. "Head Witch, it's a pleasure to meet you."

She'd addressed Mum, not me. I cleared my throat. "Excuse me. I am the Head Witch."

Tension zipped up my spine when she gave me an assessing look. "You're Head Witch, are you? Interesting choice. I am Isadora Feverfew."

She shook my hand firmly enough that I held back a wince. "Robin Wildwood. Pleasure to meet you."

Isadora then repeated the greeting with the others, all of whom appeared just as wary of the newcomer as I was, with the exception of Acacia, who simply glowered at everyone.

Mum stepped behind me and spoke in a low murmur. "Go on, invite them in."

"Do the rest of the council know the meeting will be early?" I whispered to Mum.

"Yes," she said out of the corner of her mouth. "Stick to the plan. We'll talk later."

"We're several hours *ahead* of our plan." Did she have enough activities on the list to entertain all the Head Witches for hours, or would we just have to sit awkwardly in the meeting room until the workday ended?

Mum didn't reply, but the Head Witches, having finished their introductions, looked expectantly at us. Or rather, at me.

"Welcome to the Wildwood Coven's headquarters." I gestured to the door. "The meeting will be held in here."

I led the way through the lobby to the designated meeting room, where I took a seat at the head of the table. The other Head Witches then filed into the room and sat down, along with their accompanying council members and assistants. While the Head Witches claimed leadership, nobody could entirely forget that the other council members were elected coven leaders who might find themselves holding a sceptre of their own in the future, and anyone who discounted their opinions was asking for trouble.

As for me, I was more relieved that I wouldn't be expected to do all the talking and that my fellow coven members were allowed to attend, including Chloe, who I'd instructed to take notes on my behalf. The very last people to enter the room were Aunt Shannon and Vanessa, her oldest daughter, who sat down at the far end of the table, as close to the door as possible. Perhaps they intended to sneak out at the first opportunity. I wouldn't have objected if they did, but then again, if I couldn't escape this meeting, I'd make sure they couldn't either.

When everyone was seated, silence descended upon the table.

"For those of you who are new here, let me take the time to welcome you to Wildwood Heath," I said. "It's an honour for my coven to host this meeting, and I hope it can be a good and productive start to our relationship."

The first part of the meeting was simple enough, intended to bring everyone up to speed on current events within the local magical communities. Despite my long absence, I'd already found out most of this information over the past week either via my mother or through reading the notes Chloe had given me, so I smiled and nodded while the other witches gave the rest of us a lengthy update on recent developments in their covens and communities.

Their news covered births, deaths, and major scandals such as the arrest of prominent members or people who'd gone rogue or accidentally lost their titles or got themselves cursed. Impressively, the other witches managed to make things like runaway dragons and wild spells turning people into furniture sound as dry as old paper, and I had to fight to keep from dozing off.

After the updates had finally dragged to a halt, the catering company brought in refreshments in the form of plates of sandwiches. This was a last-minute addition on Mum's part, since the others had all arrived before lunchtime and without us having made any arrangements. I had an inkling our family's chef had been roped into helping out, but the food was nice, and nobody had any complaints. Except I wouldn't have minded a trip to the café to grab a latte. The coffee provided with lunch wasn't terrible by any means, but it would have been nice to get away from the judgmental stares for a bit. Especially as half of them came from my mother. While I didn't think I'd made my boredom obvious, I foresaw a lecture on everything I'd done wrong as soon as we were behind closed doors.

When the meeting resumed, Mavis Willow announced the next topic of the day: magical laws, a subject I knew little about. Neither did Mavis, it seemed, since she let the other three Head Witches spend an hour arguing back and forth about the merits of letting vampires enforce their own laws on rogues without deferring to the Head Witches. Managing different paranormal laws could get messy to say the least, so according to Isadora Feverfew, we ought to leave well enough alone. Acacia Bracken, who seemed intent on arguing with everyone else for the sake of it, disagreed.

"Those paranormal hunters are exactly what we need here in the Midlands," she said. "Keeping those other paranormals in line shouldn't be our job, but we can't trust them to police themselves either."

"Says who?" Isadora responded. "It's worked fine for the past few hundred years without us needing to bring in trigger-happy outsiders."

I had to agree with Isadora on that one. From what I gathered, the paranormal hunters were an organisation formed of ordinary humans in the know about the magical world, and they'd suffered a recent scandal when one of their branches had turned out to be secretly run by a power-mad fairy with a grudge against the covens. That was reason enough not to let them into our town as far as I was concerned.

For most of the afternoon, Isadora and Acacia argued back and forth while everyone else waited for them to tire out. Aunt Shannon didn't speak at all, and neither did Vanessa. I couldn't figure out if she'd walked in with an agenda, but given her habit of attempting to undermine my authority as Head Witch, I had little doubt that she'd considered how she might turn this meeting to her own advantage.

Finally, Mum gave me a faint nod across the table, a signal to call the meeting to an end. I did so, silencing Isadora and Acacia's argument, and politely offered a tour of the town to anyone who wanted to get out and explore while it was still light outside.

To my consternation, all the other Head Witches said yes, and so did most of the council members. Not all of them. Aunt Shannon and Vanessa were the first people out the door, while Chloe ducked back into my office to type up the notes for the meeting.

That left Mum and me to lead the others towards the woodland path, where I let Mum take the lead and waited for Tansy to catch up to me. She scampered up my arm and perched on my shoulder.

"So those are the Head Witches," she whispered in my ear. "Not that impressive, are they?"

"Shh."

"What? They can't understand me."

"True, but Mum will probably say it's bad manners for me to talk to you behind their backs."

Tansy scoffed. "Like they wouldn't do the same in your place."

"Speaking of familiars, have you seen that magpie?"

"Nope. Why, was Aunt Shannon throwing her weight around in the meeting?"

"No, she didn't say a word." Despite that, I refused to believe she wasn't plotting to take advantage of having so many VIP guests in town. No doubt in a way that would paint me in a bad light.

Still, despite the arguments, the first meeting hadn't gone too badly. After the tour, the other Head Witches would check into the inn at which they'd be staying for the night. While we weren't directly responsible for their accommodations, we'd still be on the hook for any complaints they might have. They didn't look too impressed with the Wildwood either.

Tansy shifted on my shoulder, her fur standing on end. "Something feels weird in here."

"In what way?"

As I walked around a corner, a sudden loud croak came from near my feet, and I jumped high enough to smack my head on a low branch.

"Who's there?" Rubbing my forehead, I peered into the bushes at my feet and spied a bright-green toad. Mavis Willow's familiar. Helena, she'd called her.

"Help!" croaked Helena. "Something terrible has happened. I think she's dead."

"Who?" I straightened upright while the toad hopped out of the bushes towards a clearing. Tansy clung to my shoulder, and I followed at a soft tread. No birdsong filled the trees, and ahead of us, a young witch lay in a tangle of branches. Any doubts that she was dead disappeared when I saw the blood. Something with sharp claws had set upon her, and I averted my gaze, nauseated.

What had attacked her? An image of a dragon appeared in my mind's eye, but I pushed it aside. Yes, my family and I had reunited a baby dragon with its parents on our way home, but we'd released it into the wild far south of the Wildwood. Dragons didn't make their homes in forests, preferring areas with plenty of space to spread their wings. Something else was responsible for this attack—but what?

"Robin?" Mum called out. "Head Witch? Are you there?"

Even when she was yelling at me, she maintained her fake tone of deference and concern. It was more than a little jarring at a time like this, but I turned my back on the body and followed the sound of her voice. "Mum, someone's dead. A witch. I think she was attacked by some kind of beast."

"A beast?" echoed another Head Witch.

I hadn't intended to make this public, but the clearing was wide open. I was surprised only Mavis's familiar had found the body before I had.

Mum's expression was utterly blank. "Show me."

Everyone followed me into the clearing, where I stopped short of the fallen witch and faced my mother. "Does anyone know who she is?"

The witch was unfamiliar to me, though I didn't know everyone in Wildwood Heath. I was pretty sure she wasn't a member of my coven, but if she wasn't local, we were looking at a new set of problems.

Mum's gaze passed over her, her mouth a grim line. "Her name is Rachel Whitten. She's a member of the Henbane Coven."

The word *Henbane* ricocheted through my mind, but the other Head Witches didn't react to the name. They crowded around the body, whispering to one another and speculating on what kind of creature might have afflicted such horrific wounds. Their morbid curiosity made me twitchy, but Mum gave me a firm look, and it took a minute for me to realise she wanted me to take command and order the others to leave the dead witch alone. They'd have to comply since I was of equal authority with them and we were in my coven's home, but that didn't make me any keener to interrupt the gossiping witches. Still, someone had to act.

"Get away from the body," I ordered everyone. "This is a matter for the police to deal with."

Mum already had her phone in her hand and had no doubt fired off a message to Ramsey, but the Head Witches showed no signs of wanting to vacate the forest. Disregarding my order, Isadora walked over to the body and raised her sceptre.

"What are you doing?" I tensed, my grip tightening on my own sceptre. Somehow, despite all our preparations, Mum and I hadn't considered that I might end up in a standoff with my fellow Head Witches over a dead body.

"Identifying the cause of the wounds," she responded. "Claws, it looks like."

"That's the police's job," I told her at a prompting glare from Mum's direction. While it was a welcome change from gritting my teeth and keeping quiet, I knew better than to think I'd done anything to earn her apparent submission to my authority. This was all part of the act, nothing more.

Acacia stepped in, her own sceptre at the ready. "It's got to be a manticore attack."

"No, a wyvern," said Isadora.

"That's enough." I gave the faintest flick of my sceptre, and a flash of purple light enveloped the clearing. When everyone looked at me, I said, "You're all walking on a crime scene. The police will be here at any moment, and if you're waving your sceptres over the body, then they'll have no choice but to treat you as they would anyone else who stumbled upon a dead witch in the woods. Step aside."

To my intense relief, Ramsey's voice rang through the trees before anyone could argue. "This is the police. What's going on here?"

The others reluctantly backed away to leave a path for my brother to enter the clearing. He didn't have his team with him, which suggested he'd run straight here from home the instant he'd got Mum's message, but my warning and his uniform got the message across. Ramsey looked down at the dead girl, his mouth twisting into a grimace. "She was attacked, you say?"

"Yes, I believe she was," said Mum. "Are the rest of your team members on their way?"

"Yes, they are." He faced the other Head Witches. "Everyone except the police should leave the crime scene."

Mutters arose, mostly from Isadora and Acacia, who weren't thrilled at being ordered around.

I had trouble feeling sorry for them when someone was dead, and not by accident. Magical wildlife didn't just wander up to town and attack members of the public. Yes, we lived near a magical forest, but incidents like this one were almost unheard of.

"Someone did this on purpose," I murmured to Tansy as we led the way out of the forest. She remained perched on my shoulder, her tail quivering, as if the creature had freaked her out as much as the rest of us. "Not just the attack. They wanted the Head Witches to find her body."

"Was that your aunt's master plan?" Tansy remarked. "I wonder if that's what her magpie was doing while you were in the meeting room?"

Aunt Shannon? "I don't know, Tansy. We thought she was a murderer once before and turned out to be mistaken, remember?"

"The murder might not have been intentional," Tansy suggested. "Maybe she just wanted to set a giant monster loose in the forest to cause a bit of harmless chaos. You know, trample a few trees, scare a tourist or two, and make everyone think we're irresponsible and the Wildwood is dangerous."

"And it was pure bad luck that someone happened to be in the monster's path?" The idea had merit, I had to admit, but the identity of the victim was hard to ignore. "A Henbane witch? I don't know if that can be put down to luck."

Mum fell into step with me. "I think we should take the Head Witches to their accommodation and leave them to settle in before we continue the tour tomorrow."

My mouth parted. "If you're sure. I didn't think they needed a tour, since most of them have been here before. I wish we'd skipped the whole thing."

That way, they wouldn't have been with us when we'd discovered the body. As it was, I had no doubt they'd be on the phone to the rest of their covens at the first opportunity.

"You think they wouldn't have found out anyway?" Mum asked. "Expecting to keep this quiet was absurd."

"I never said I did." So much for avoiding an argument. "I'm not a Seer. Even I didn't plan for mysterious bodies turning up in the woods. Did you?"

"Robin." She lowered her voice. "I would ask you to comport yourself appropriately until we are alone."

"We *are* alone." The other Head Witches were walking so slowly that they'd almost fallen out of sight—except for Jemima, whose harried posture suggested she wanted to get out of the forest as fast as possible. "Do you have a plan to make sure none of them leaves the inn to come poking around the woods again?"

"Yes, I do," she said. "Ramsey will station his fellow officers at the main entrances to the woodland path. On that subject, I'd prefer it if you didn't go back into the forest yourself, Robin. This is not a matter for the Head Witch to deal with."

Translation: we had to leave this in Ramsey's hands.

Which I was all too happy to do, except that the possibility of Aunt Shannon's involvement refused to leave my mind.

"Whoever did this... they wanted to give a bad impression of our coven as well as the rest of the town," I told her. "You agree with me on that, right?"

She said nothing, simply walking alongside me out of the woods and down the high street. When we reached the Owl's Nest Inn, where each of the Head Witches had their own private room, the two of us waited to be sure none of them would try to follow us back into the forest before leaving.

When I veered towards the forest myself, however, Mum stopped walking. "Didn't I tell you to leave the crime scene alone?"

"Not in so many words, you didn't." I didn't particularly want another argument, but all my instincts told me that the murder was directly tied to the presence of the other Head Witches. "I want to find out who did this. There are a fair few people who'd have reason to derail our gathering, such as certain family members of ours who left the meeting early."

Mum began walking again. "I do hope nobody is listening in, including their familiars."

"They aren't." Tansy spoke for the first time since we'd gone to the inn, and she still hadn't let go of my shoulder. "That magpie was missing for the whole meeting. She didn't come to chase me around the garden once. What's the betting she was leading our mysterious monster through the forest?"

"I wouldn't be so quick to blame my sister," Mum warned. "This attack doesn't seem like her style. It's impersonal, indirect, and nearly impossible to blame on one of us."

"It'd explain what she's been doing for the past week while we weren't here," I pointed out. "She had days to put together her plan and set that creature loose in the forest. Whether she intended for someone to get killed or not, the idea of a beast running amok in the Wildwood is enough to terrify most people."

"I don't disagree, Robin," Mum said, "but I'd advise you to keep those thoughts to yourself until we have more proof. Think of the scandal it would cause if the Head Witches realised the person responsible for this might be a member of the same coven hosting the meeting, and the Head Witch's own family at that."

Typical. "I'd be more than happy to avoid mentioning any of this in front of them, provided you drop the act the rest of the time. It's making me itchy."

"Me too," said Tansy. "Anyway, I bet all those Head Witches are happily accusing one another already."

We slowed our pace when we neared the clearing, where several police officers blocked our path.

"It's just me—and Robin," Mum told them. "The other Head Witches are at their place of accommodation, and none of them followed us back."

"Good." Ramsey approached us. "We estimate the girl was killed up to an hour ago. The creature responsible for the attack must still be in the area, but it's going to take a considerable effort to search the forest."

"Your team can't search the entire Wildwood," I pointed out. "Also, who's going to investigate who set it loose in the first place?"

"There's no proof that anyone did."

"We know that creature didn't get in here by accident," Tansy interjected. "Someone brought it here, and I for one want it out of the forest before it frightens all the birds away."

Ramsey exhaled in a sigh. "Look, we have to prioritise finding the creature in the interests of public safety. We've looked around the crime scene, but so far, we haven't found any obvious clues as to what we're dealing with."

"Why not ask the wildlife?" I suggested. "I can guarantee anything else living in the forest will have seen the intruder."

In fact, they might have also seen the person who'd set it loose. Then again, if this was Aunt Shannon's work, she had the same ability to influence and communicate with animals as I did, and she was too smart not to factor our shared talent into her plans. It was worth a shot, so I looked around for any animals who might talk. Yet the surrounding trees remained empty of any birds, and the usual sounds of woodland creatures were absent. No birdsong, no rustling in the bushes, and even the breeze seemed hushed. It was as if all living creatures had entirely vacated this area of the forest.

"The animals aren't going to come out as long as we're tramping around," Ramsey asserted. "Besides, we need to remove the body, which also means reporting Rachel's death to her family and to her coven."

Oh boy. I'd forgotten someone would have to break the bad news to the Henbane Coven's leader, Tiffany. Our coven's history with the Henbanes was rocky to say the least. A few weeks ago, Tiffany had tried to recruit my cousin Rowan to her coven's ranks by taking advantage of the desperation to get away from her toxic family members, and while I'd forgiven Rowan for the interview she'd been bullied into doing with the press, the Henbanes were another story. Oh, and there was the tiny fact that someone from their coven had also tried to assassinate me a few weeks ago. While we'd never proved a definite link to Tiffany herself, I doubted she'd been completely oblivious. She'd kept her distance in order to save her own skin, and while she'd taken no interest in meeting the other Head Witches, she wouldn't stay on the sidelines now one of her fellow coven members was dead.

"I'll tell Tiffany," Mum offered. "She'll be furious, of course, but the news might sting less coming from me than from Robin."

As if I'd *asked* Tiffany's wayward relatives to try to bump me off. "And Rachel's family?"

"I'll call them myself," said Ramsey. "Once we've removed her body from the crime scene. Some of my team will stay here to keep an eye on things and to have a look for the creature responsible, as it's still a potential danger to anyone who ventures into the woods."

"How are you going to warn everyone?" I asked. "Stick up signs on the trees warning people to stay out of the woods? I don't see the werewolves going for that."

"I'll manage," he answered. "As for you, I wouldn't linger in here."

His tone grated on me, but I hadn't the energy for another conflict. I hoped he knew what he was doing, because a lot of people lived on the edges of the Wildwood. Like our dad, for instance. In fact, our family's garden backed onto the forest, and even the Sky Hopper team's practice field was outside of the town's boundaries.

If whoever had planned this had intended to cause as much disruption as possible, they'd certainly succeeded.

"I won't," I told my brother. "I'm going back to the office."

He gave me an incredulous look. "You're going to work? Really? It's the end of the day."

He didn't need to tell *me* that. "The Head Witches arrived hours early, and I need to sort out a few things before I head home."

His incredulity turned to suspicion. "Like what? You can't get involved in this, Robin."

"I think someone needs to let Aunt Shannon know, don't you?"

"*She* won't be at the office," Mum said, overhearing. "I'd go home, Robin."

Honestly. She'd spent weeks lecturing me for wanting to use my leisure hours to relax, yet she chose now of all times to make an objection.

"I will, once I've made sure Chloe has left." I wasn't lying. In fact, I wouldn't have been surprised if she felt the need to stay all night as penance for taking a week off. "See you both later."

Without waiting for a reply, I departed the crime scene, hoping that Aunt Shannon *was* at the office so I could gauge her reaction to the news. Guilty or not, I would have liked to find out *what* was loose in the woods, and it did not seem as if my brother had that question ranked as a priority.

"Aunt Shannon's gone too far this time," Tansy said in my ear. "The whole forest feels *wrong*."

"I'm still not a hundred percent sure it's her doing though."

One thing was clear. Whoever was responsible had intended to make both me *and* the Wildwood Coven look incompetent at best. Even if you ignored the esteem of our visitors, anyone would be reluctant to visit Wildwood Heath if word got out that there were monsters loose in the woods. If Aunt Shannon had genuinely set some unknown magical beast loose right behind her own home, she'd taken a major risk of her plan backfiring in her face.

"If not this, she'll have been cooking something up this week," Tansy said. "Otherwise, I'd blame the Henbanes, but would even Tiffany kill one of her own coven members?"

She didn't mind sending one to jail, I thought. "Though I suppose we can't rule out one of the other Head Witches having brought a monstrous friend along to ruin our day."

Had the crime been concocted from within the town or outside of it? There was no way to know for certain as long as the creature remained at large, so I'd have to start by identifying *what* was currently rampaging around the forest.

4

As I approached the witches' headquarters, I sent Tansy to look for any signs of Aunt Shannon lurking around.

"She isn't in." Tansy scampered back to my side. "No surprise there. She's probably preparing her cover story."

"Figures." I went to my own office instead. As I'd suspected, Chloe was still at her desk, typing away on her laptop.

"I know it's the end of the workday," Chloe said to me with barely a glance up from her work. "I just wanted to finish these notes… what happened to you?"

Did I really look that bad? Thanks to my trek into the woods, I did have mud all over my best cloak, but I assumed it was my face she'd reacted to. "We found a dead body in the woods."

Chloe jumped to her feet, nearly knocking over her laptop. "You what?"

Grandma appeared in a flash. "Assassins? Again?"

"Not assassins. Some kind of monster." I walked past

my grandmother's ghost to the bookshelves that lined the wall on one side of the office. "That's why I came back here. I assume you have resources on magical monsters."

"Monster?" Chloe echoed. "What—how can there be a monster in the Wildwood?"

"Because someone put it there," I replied. "Or set it loose. Same difference."

"Who did it kill?" Grandma demanded. "Was it one of our coven members?"

"No… one of the Henbanes," I told them both. "I noticed Aunt Shannon isn't around. She was awfully quick to leave the meeting too."

"She'll have gone home," Chloe said, apparently not picking up on the implied meaning in my words. "This beast though… if it killed a Henbane witch, then who's going to tell them?"

"My mother is," I said. "As for me? I'd like to know *what* someone set loose in the woods before it attacks anyone else."

"What are you doing?" Grandma floated over as I started taking down books from the shelves. "Put those back."

"Your books aren't decorations, Grandma." I found a likely title—*The Advanced Guide to Magical Beasts*—and tucked it under my arm. "They're intended to help the Head Witch with any problems she might encounter. Did you ever run into any monsters in the woods in all the years you were Head Witch?"

"Define 'monster.'" Grandma followed me to the desk, where I put down the book.

"Magical beast then." I flipped open the book and scanned the list of magical beasts, of which there were close to a hundred. *Yeah... I might need to narrow this down a little.* "I have a hard time believing nobody heard or saw anything, given how close to town the attack took place."

"I'll help." Chloe sprang over to examine the bookshelves and scanned the available titles. "I'm not an expert on magical beasts, but I did take a module in magical tracking as part of my degree. From what I remember, the easiest way to identify a creature is by looking at its footprints. Did you see any?"

"No, but I was too busy trying to keep the other Head Witches from trampling all over the crime scene." I flipped to the first page of the textbook, titled *Dragons and Wyverns*. Thanks for that one, universe. "I didn't have my camera with me, but I can go and snap some photos later."

"You most certainly will not," Grandma said. "Isn't your brother in charge of the investigation? That should be his job, not yours."

"Yes, he is, but that doesn't mean I can't help him out." I lifted my head from the textbook to look at my grandmother's ghost. "It's personal, Grandma. The person who did this intended to paint a target on our coven *and* on our family. Do you want to help me or not?"

A scowl creased her wrinkled face. "I can't go into the Wildwood myself. I've tried, but I can only get as far as the back door of my house."

"We'll work with it." So that was her limit. Good to know for future reference, at least, though I'd hoped her decades of experience would be able to give me a clue as to how to handle this latest disaster. My long-forgotten lessons on magical creatures at the academy certainly weren't enough to prepare me to identify whatever had killed Rachel, so I closed the textbook. "I'll get my camera and see if I can snap some photos of its footprints."

"Want me to help?" Chloe asked. "Though I'm not sure your mother and brother will want us showing up at the crime scene…"

"You can go home," I told her. "I'll convince my brother to let me snap some pictures, and I'll bring them to the office tomorrow."

"If you're sure."

"I am." I made for the door, the textbook tucked under one arm and my sceptre in the other hand. "I don't want you working unnecessary overtime. We have a long day ahead of us tomorrow."

"Yes, you do," Grandma cut in. "You should be preparing for your next meeting, not investigating magical monsters."

"I can do both." It would have been nice if she'd offered more help, but there was a limit on what anyone could do without access to the crime scene. The notion of her haunting the forest would probably have put off most monsters though.

When I reached the house, I unlocked the door and made straight for the stairs to fetch my camera before anyone waylaid me.

"Robin?" Mum called up the stairs behind me, to no surprise.

"Yes?" I ducked into my room, grabbed the camera in my free hand, and returned to the stairs to find Mum waiting in the hallway.

"Where are you going?"

"Not to the Fox's Den, don't worry."

"I'd rather you were going to the pub than the forest,

Robin."

I held up the camera. "I only wanted to snap a couple of pictures of the creature's footprints, if there are any. I got a textbook from the office on magical monsters, but I need some clues first."

She tutted. "So that's why you went back to work."

I rolled my eyes. "I did have to turf Chloe out before she spent the whole night working. Anyway, I bet the police don't have Grandma's resources."

"They will when your brother comes home." She stepped aside. "Fine. If you're going to the forest, then you can tell him yourself."

"I will, don't worry." I'd won that round, so I left the house, Tansy scurrying alongside me towards the woodland path.

"I can't believe she said yes," I remarked to her. "Though my photos did come in handy in the last investigation I ended up involved in."

Tansy made no reply. Her tail stuck up in the air, her posture was agitated, and I reached to let her scramble up my arm to my shoulder.

"Can you smell the creature?" I asked her. "Is that what's bothering you?"

"No, I can't smell anything," she replied. "That's why it's so creepy."

"Huh." I didn't have Tansy's refined senses, so I didn't know what to make of that one. "Grandma's books should be able to help us figure out what kind of creature it is then reel it in."

And find out who brought it here and set it loose in the forest. If the police hadn't found any clues at the scene, they'd had little choice but to put the search for the human perpetrator on hold. After all, if they ignored the monster loose in the woods, they ran the risk of another attack, and whoever had brought it here seemingly hadn't cared who might get caught in its path.

When I reached the entrance to the woodland path, two police officers barred my way.

"Head Witch," said a burly wizard with a crew cut. "Sorry, we're not allowed to let anyone near the scene of the crime."

"That's all right. I'm here to talk to my brother." I held up my camera. "I'm looking into identifying the creature responsible, so I need to snap a few photos."

"Ramsey didn't mention that." He folded his arms across his chest. "He *did* tell us not to let any Head Witches into the forest."

"I'm not one of the Head Witches from out of town." I dropped my voice. "I also don't want them telling everyone in the magical world we have wild beasts running amok in the forest. All I need is a picture, and I can help identify the creature."

The two officers exchanged looks, then they shuffled to either side to let me pass. I walked the short distance down the path to the clearing where the attack had taken place. Ramsey, who stood near the place where the witch's body had lain, spotted me at once. His annoyance turned to confusion when he saw my camera. "What are you doing this time?"

"Has the creature left any footprints?" I asked. "Chloe told me footprints are the best way to identify the attacker."

"There aren't any." He ran a hand through his blond curls, his expression rattled. "There's a lot of trampled undergrowth but no actual markings left by the creature."

"What about on the ground?" I trod closer to the tangled undergrowth and snapped a couple of photos of the clearing. "Or on the nearby trees? It must have left some kind of trail when it left the clearing."

"Not that we've been able to find—yet," he said. "We're searching the forest, but it'll get dark soon. We'll wait for the medical reports from the hospital when they've examined the girl's body—that ought to give us a better idea of what we're up against."

I didn't argue with that, though I couldn't shake the feeling that there ought to be more evidence here at the scene. Like bait the culprit had used to lure the creature closer to town or clues pointing to their identity. I took a few more photos—some of which Tansy insisted on photobombing—and ignored Ramsey's mutters that I was wasting my time.

When I'd finished, I said, "If you want to read Grandma's books on magical monsters, then I brought one home with me. I'll let Mum know you're on your way back."

Without waiting for a reply, I left the clearing. Tansy snickered on my shoulder. "He looks like he trod on Prickles."

"If I'd known all I needed to do to get my way was talk louder than him, I'd have started much sooner."

Not strictly true, but I was perfectly willing to annoy my brother if it meant getting closer to finding the person responsible for the attack. Preferably before it rebounded upon our coven and on Wildwood Heath as a whole.

When I got home, Tansy jumped off my shoulder and

followed me into the hallway. Mum loomed out of the living room when I pulled out my camera to check the photos I'd taken and nearly caused me to drop it. "Whoa, Mum."

"You'll need to print those." Mum indicated my camera. "I'll get the printer set up."

"What?" Wait, she was offering to help? I'd half expected her to reprimand me for bothering Ramsey or at least putting the crime before our guests as the topmost priority for this week. This was new. "Really?"

She held out a hand. "Give me the camera, and I'll sort them out."

Huh. Who would have thought all it'd take to bring us together was a deadly monster being set loose in the woods?

"Thanks." I handed over the camera. "Ah… do you have any ideas about who might be behind this?"

"Do you?"

Hmm. Maybe she was still a little annoyed with me after all, unless she genuinely wanted to know what I thought. "Pretty much everyone who wants me out of my position as Head Witch—and who knew about this week's meeting. The timing isn't coincidental."

Mum's lips pursed. "Well, try not to accuse any of the other Head Witches. We don't want to start any feuds."

Yeah… I think someone already did.

———

After a near-sleepless night, the last thing I wanted was to return to the office for another meeting with the Head Witches. Mum had kept her word and printed out all the photos I'd taken, but I hadn't been able to draw any conclusions from them—except that my familiar was ridiculously photogenic. Giving up, I'd handed the pictures that Tansy hadn't ruined to my brother and then gone to bed.

Ramsey himself was still waiting for the medical reports on the victim's body, as far as I knew, but magical monsters weren't his area of expertise. Nor mine either, but it would have been a lot easier if I didn't have to waste half my day sitting in meetings while keeping up the impression of complete control in front of the other Head Witches. As opposed to sneaking around trying to find magical monsters—at least not where the other Head Witches could see.

Tansy's usual morning activity was to chase the local birds around the garden, but she came back into the kitchen when I was eating breakfast.

"There's nobody at the bird feeder," she remarked. "Only a few clueless pigeons from the other side of town who have no idea about the attack in the forest."

"You'd think one of the local birds would have seen the monster." I took a bite of toast. "There's got to be a witness, surely."

"None of the birds would talk to me." Tansy hopped onto the table and stole a piece of my toast. "I suppose I do chase them around a lot."

"Yes, you do." Something wasn't right though. The monster's arrival must have caused a stir, and there couldn't be no wildlife left in the Wildwood to tell tales. Knowing Ramsey, he'd have officers patrolling the main routes into the forest day and night, but none of them shared our gift.

I needed to be at the office in less than two hours, but I grabbed another piece of toast to go and went into the back garden. Tansy followed, taking a half-hearted swipe at the bird feeder from below, and someone called my name from behind the flowerbeds. "Robin?"

I quickened my steps and found Piper, my best friend and the coven's gardener, up to her elbows in mulch. "Hey, Piper. I guess you heard?"

Her brow wrinkled. "How long were you back in town before you found another dead body? Only you, Robin."

"Technically, it wasn't me who found her… and she wasn't killed by a person." I glanced over at the mass of trees at the back of the garden, my spine prickling. "The killer was some kind of magical beast, which is presumably still at large."

"Yeah, and I've never seen so little wildlife around," she said. "It's like a ghost town in the woods. Wait, wrong word. Ghost forest?"

"I think ghosts are less scary." Even the garden was bereft of the sound of birdsong. "Tansy said the same. I hoped I might find a local animal or two who saw the attack."

"They probably ran for it," Piper replied. "They'll be back."

"Not as long as the creature is still around," Tansy put in. "Which it must be. It's too quiet."

My heart gave an uneasy skip. "My brother's team searched until it got dark, but they can't cover the whole forest, even in the daytime. Especially when they don't actually know what they're looking for yet."

"Not a dragon?" asked Piper.

"No." I frowned. "Where'd you hear that?"

"I didn't. You went to help a dragon find its parents when you were out of town, right?"

"Yes, but we moved them to a colony that was miles south of here," I said. "They don't live in enclosed places without open skies. Not everyone knows that, so I guess I should avoid mentioning it."

It'd be a convenient way to point the finger in my family's direction, but the person who'd brought the monster to town couldn't possibly have known we'd had an unplanned detour. Regardless, unwanted rumours were the last thing we needed.

"Robin?" Mum called to me from near the back door. "You aren't going into the forest, are you?"

So much for our new truce. "I'll tell you the rest of it later."

Piper grinned. "Including your date with Harvey yesterday?"

"Don't expect me to get a moment's peace until our visitors are gone," I warned her. "Also, can you let me know if any of the wildlife comes back?"

"Will do," she said.

I returned to Mum's side. "No, I'm not going into the forest. Is Ramsey already at the police station?"

"Yes, and the last I heard, so was Tiffany," she replied. "Apparently, she was there for hours, demanding to know what killed her coven member."

"Seriously?" I blinked at her. "I thought she didn't care the last time one of her coven members got into trouble."

"The circumstances were different," Mum said. "One of her own has been a victim of a seemingly unknown attacker. That's bound to have shaken her up."

She had a point. When someone in her coven had been

trying to assassinate me, Tiffany had had to keep her distance so she wouldn't be arrested as well. Now she'd gone to the other extreme.

"She'll have to get in line," I said. "I don't doubt the police are snowed under with complaints from concerned citizens if they've told everyone in town not to go into the woods."

"There's also this." Mum held up her phone to show me an article from the *Blue Moon,* the local tabloid and the bane of my existence. The headline read, "Mystery Monster Attack Threatens New Head Witch's Gathering in Wildwood Heath."

"How on earth did the press find out?" I stared at the names attached to the article. Clarice and Speck, the same reporters I'd driven out of town weeks ago. Either they'd somehow sneaked back in, or someone had called to tell them the news.

"I can make a few guesses," Mum said. "It does no good to speculate, but we need to be ready for the tabloids to immediately react to any new developments on this case."

Wonderful. Not only did we have a murderer in town, but we also had someone who was willing to sell out their fellow witches to the press. Either they were local and happy to sacrifice the rest of town for the sake of trouncing our coven's reputation, or one of our visitors was secretly reporting everything that happened to a press contact on the outside.

"You don't think the person who brought the monster here called the press too?" I whispered, casting a glance in the direction of Aunt Shannon's house. "To ensure the story reached the right ears?"

"I wouldn't rule anything out at this stage," Mum

responded. "That said, I don't think you can put off a visit to the Henbane Coven for any longer."

I raised a brow. "To offer my condolences to Tiffany? Sure she won't throw it back in my face?"

"I've already spoken to Tiffany myself," she said. "She ought to be back at her base, and it's courteous for the Head Witch to pay her a visit."

"You know, I think I'd rather take an early meeting with the other Head Witches instead." When she gave me a stern look, I relented. "Right, I'm going."

"Good luck," Tansy called after me.

"Hey, you can't get out of this." I beckoned to her. "If I have to suffer, so do you."

"I already did." She reluctantly ran up to join me. "That creepy forest gave me nightmares."

"Does it still smell of nothing?"

"I'd need to get closer to check." She shuddered. "I think I'll pass."

After leaving the house via the front door, the pair of us walked to the Henbane Coven's headquarters. With Tansy perched on my shoulder, I braced myself and knocked on the door.

Several seconds later, Tiffany Henbane appeared in the doorway. She'd foregone her usual bright clothing for mourning black and looked sullenly at me with red-rimmed eyes. "It's you, Head Witch. I was beginning to wonder if you ever intended to show your face."

I ignored the jab. "I have a large number of responsibilities on my hands, but I came to tell you how sorry I am for the loss of Rachel. My family and I are working tirelessly to find out the cause of her death."

"Yes, that saintly brother of yours is hard at work." She

sniffed. "Driving everyone else away and insisting on pursuing the ridiculous theory of some unknown monster roaming around the woods."

"What do you think he should be doing instead?" Suspicion spiked within me. "The Wildwood is important to our entire town, and to have it labelled unsafe can only hurt us all in the long run. The sooner we capture the creature responsible for Rachel's death and apprehend the person responsible for setting it loose, the better."

She gave a wild laugh. "There's no *creature* loose in the woods. Make no mistake, a shifter is responsible."

I gaped at her. "A… shifter?"

"A werewolf," she said. "How many shifters live near the forest and run wild at the full moon? It's only natural that they'd use them as hunting grounds."

"Not against humans." Was it even the full moon? I'd have to check. Besides, most shifters were in human form ninety percent of the time anyway. Her accusation brought me up short. Tiffany never hesitated to sow discord among the other witches, so I'd never considered she might level the blame at another group of paranormals. "They're bound by the same rules as the rest of us."

"They constantly get into fights for dominance," she said. "Think about it. The attacker left no traces, did they? When they came to their senses, they turned into a human and walked away, leaving Rachel for dead."

Okay, that was enough of that. Considering my own dad and his wife lived near the forest with their two shifter kids, I didn't appreciate the accusation. I gave her a flat stare, abandoning my attempts to show sympathy. "Tiffany, I realise you're upset, but there's zero evidence that a shifter was anywhere near the scene of the attack."

"There's no evidence of magical monsters either."

"Yet," I said. "The medical reports have yet to be released. Let the police do their jobs, and please refrain from provoking enmity with the other paranormals."

She drew herself upright. "I should have guessed that would be your response. Your coven is set on ensuring that nobody else is allowed a chance at justice."

"I beg to differ." I should have known she'd point the finger straight back in my own face. "Justice for the victim is our priority, but we don't accuse anyone without proof. That's why we're assuming that nobody in *your* coven is guilty of this until further evidence comes to light. I'd appreciate it if you extended the same courtesy to the shifters."

Instead of answering, she slammed the door in my face. Should have seen that one coming.

Tansy hissed in my ear as a flutter of wings signalled a magpie taking flight nearby. I should also have guessed Aunt Shannon was spying on our conversation. *Right. She's next.*

5

I was probably pushing my luck by following Aunt Shannon's familiar after she'd witnessed my meeting with Tiffany Henbane go sideways, but the quicker I figured out if she'd been involved in the monster attack, the better. While Tansy scaled the wall to see if she was in her office, I entered the headquarters of the Wildwood Coven alone.

We didn't have a meeting scheduled with the other Head Witches until that afternoon, so it came as a surprise to find Mavis Willow and her toad familiar waiting outside my office door.

"Oh—Mavis." I halted in front of her. "Can I help you?"

I wasn't sure if I was supposed to give the customary greeting outside of a formal setting, but another thought hit me: had she been listening to my conversation with Tiffany as well?

"I was curious as to whether you found the origins of whatever attacked that poor girl yet," Mavis said. "I assume your family is looking into it, are they?"

"I'm afraid you'll have to ask my—ask the head of law enforcement." I figured mentioning my brother was in charge of the police wouldn't make me look any more competent. "They're working around the clock to find the creature."

"What kind of creature is it?" she asked. "I assume the police have searched the area for footprints."

What was her angle? "They have, but I'm waiting for an update on the identity of the creature."

Was she trying to get in on the investigation herself? Or was she simply expressing concern on behalf of the victim? I would have bet on the former, given that I was talking to a Head Witch. Even Jemima hadn't checked in on the investigation after her return to the inn, and I'd already *met* her the week before, though I wouldn't have said we were fast friends.

"I see," said Mavis. "Whatever it turns out to be, I can understand why the creature might be hard to track, given the size of the forest."

Hmm. I couldn't for the life of me figure out if her tone was genuine. "Perhaps, but my family has an affinity with magical creatures, and I have no doubt we'll be able to find it. That said, I would welcome anyone who has pertinent information to come forwards and share it with the police—or with myself or my mother if that's more convenient."

"I have no information," she said. "I was simply curious as to your progress... I used to be apprenticed to a tracker myself."

"Oh." Now I felt like a fool for assuming she had ulterior motives. I'd been spending too much time around my grandmother's ghost. "Ah, I think the police will send me an update on their progress before the meeting."

"I see." She made for the door. "I'll see you later, Head Witch."

"Enjoy your morning." *And please don't go into the forest,* I added silently. Expert or not, I didn't need to worry about anyone else being attacked by our mysterious creature.

I might have blamed my family members for instilling enough paranoia in me that I immediately assumed everyone was plotting against me, but recent experience had taught me it wasn't unfounded. Mavis might have simply been curious, but a former tracker's apprentice would certainly have known how to bring an unknown creature into the forest without being seen. Regardless, my main suspect remained Aunt Shannon, who was no doubt listening to her familiar's report on my conversation with Tiffany right this instant. I put Mavis out of my mind and waited for my familiar to return.

Within a minute, Tansy came running downstairs, having presumably hopped through an open window on the upper floor. "Your aunt's upstairs, and she's alone."

"Perfect." Or not, given that I hadn't exactly rehearsed what I was going to say to her. "I wonder if Vanessa's helping her out."

"I can guarantee she is." Tansy ran up the banister as I climbed the stairs to the upper floor of the coven's headquarters. "She's probably been set up to take the fall, knowing your aunt."

"That's a bit much even for her, but I wouldn't be surprised if Vanessa's the one running around doing all her dirty work." Regardless, I didn't think Aunt Shannon would risk the arrest of her eldest—and favourite— daughter. More likely, she was doing all she could to erase all proof of either of them being linked with the creature's appearance.

Once I'd reached the upper floor, I walked towards the wooden door emblazoned with my aunt's name and rapped on the surface with my knuckles. No reply. After my second knock, I called out, "This is the Head Witch. I know you're in, Aunt Shannon."

Another pause, and then the door opened a fraction. Behind Aunt Shannon's irate expression, I glimpsed an office in as much of a state of disarray as Grandma's, but my aunt glided outside and closed the door behind her before I could get a proper look. *Is the proof in her office?* If so, then I might send Tansy to snoop around. If my aunt hadn't squirrel-proofed her office, which was a distinct possibility.

"What is it, Head Witch?" Aunt Shannon asked, injecting as much disdain as possible into the last two words.

"I wanted to talk to you alone before the others arrive." I decided to skip the preamble. "I'm sure you heard of the attack on one of the Henbane witches in the forest yesterday, and I assume your familiar has already briefed you on Tiffany's response when I went to express my condolences."

"Indeed." She looked down at me. "You think yourself capable of solving this yourself?"

"I never claimed anything of the sort," I said. "I'm sure your familiar has already conveyed everything I said to Mavis Willow when I was downstairs as well."

She gave a laugh without any humour. "You've

certainly adapted quicker than I expected, but that won't help you. The other Head Witches will eat you alive."

"Was that a reference to the beast roaming in the woods?" I enquired. "If you have any knowledge of its identity, I'd be grateful if you shared the information with the police. It's in the interests of safety for every person in Wildwood Heath that the creature is recaptured as soon as possible."

"A pretty speech," she said. "I quite agree… it paints a poor image of our coven and our town as a whole for us to allow such a tragedy to go unpunished."

"Then I'm sure you'll let me know—or my mother—if you have any information to pass on to the police." I tried to read her expression, but my aunt was a closed book at the best of times. Even if she hadn't been responsible for bringing the creature to town, she'd almost certainly seen the article in the *Blue Moon* that morning. "I'd certainly prefer for us to find the creature before we gain any more unpleasant publicity. Wouldn't you?"

"I quite agree," she said. "Though I'm surprised you haven't used the opportunity to ask for the aid of our visitors. Mavis Willow is quite the expert on magical beasts herself."

Is she now? Of course, Aunt Shannon would know since she'd had numerous meetings with the other Head Witches over the years and no doubt knew every one of their idiosyncrasies. That also meant there was a depressingly high chance she knew exactly who'd brought in the creature without needing to have been responsible for it herself. In fact, she might even have conspired *with* another Head Witch to arrange the attack—but surely

Aunt Shannon wouldn't go as far as to conspire with another coven to undermine her own.

No, she was more likely to have trusted nobody but her eldest daughter to help her out, and I'd have more of a chance of tricking a confession out of Vanessa than my Aunt Shannon.

"Interesting," I commented. "I'm sure this afternoon's meeting will give me the opportunity to get to know my guests. I assume you'll be there, and so will Vanessa?"

"Naturally." The hint of a smile curled her lip. "I hope the other Head Witches haven't made assumptions about your fitness to lead, given the timing of the attack. One would wonder why you took them into the forest, knowing the potential risks."

"Potential risks?" I echoed. "Even if they hadn't set foot in the forest themselves, they'd know of the attack by now, thanks to the person who shared the details with the press."

"You're truly surprised?" She shook her head. "How much you have to learn."

"I'm not surprised someone told tales," I said flatly. "I *was* intrigued by the names attached to the interview, given that I made it clear that Clarice and Speck aren't welcome in Wildwood Heath. I assume contacting those particular journalists was a deliberate choice on behalf of the person who did the interview."

My pointed stare was met with an expression of incredulity with a hint of amusement. "Perhaps, but it says more about your own ability to exert your authority than the interviewee, doesn't it?"

It was her. She did the interview. If she'd also set the beast loose, though, I hadn't a clue.

"If you know of a spell that can prevent anyone in town from telephoning journalists, then I think my mother, for one, would be grateful if you told her." I'd about had it with her nonsense. "Also, if your familiar overhears any information that points to the origin of the attack, you know where my office is."

"Of course." She spoke in cloyingly sweet tones that were as false as my own smile in return before I turned my back on her.

No open accusations. Not yet. Also, I should probably give Rowan a heads-up. She wouldn't be surprised in the least to learn her mother had been up to her usual tricks, but setting monsters loose in the woods was a bit much even for Aunt Shannon.

I descended the stairs and entered my own office. Chloe already sat at her desk, with Carmilla napping in her usual patch of sunlight.

"Hey, Chloe." I closed the door behind me. "What's on the agenda for this morning?"

"Admin," she replied. "Where've you been?"

"I went to talk to my aunt." I sat down at my own desk and moved a new swathe of paperwork aside. "Right after visiting the head of the Henbane Coven. I've already had my fill of duplicity for one day, and we haven't even got to the meeting yet."

"You went to talk to Tiffany Henbane?" she asked. "How was she?"

"Irrational," I replied. "She's got it into her head that a *shifter* killed Rachel. I have absolutely no idea why she jumped to that conclusion, though I suppose I should be glad she didn't blame me instead."

Her brow wrinkled. "I heard she was at the police

station for hours yesterday, complaining about not being taken seriously."

"Yeah, she's decided our coven is conspiring against her and that she can't trust any of us." I shrugged. "I might have felt sorry for her if I didn't remember how she sent an *assassin* after me a few weeks ago."

"She's playing for pity," Chloe said. "Mark my words, she'll be primed to take advantage of this situation whether she planned it or not."

"Figures," I muttered. "Oh, and Mavis Willow was here as well. According to Aunt Shannon, she's something of an expert on magical monsters. She wanted to know how far I'd got with the investigation, and I told her that the police were handling it."

"Good," she said. "Strange. Do you think she was offering her help?"

"If she was, I can't let another Head Witch in on this." Especially when Aunt Shannon had suggested I accept her help. "Imagine what Mum would say if she found out. It's bad enough that the other Head Witches know how clueless we are about the actual identity of our mysterious monster."

"If you teamed up with the other Head Witches, it'd be easier to find a solution, but I understand why you don't want to take the risk." Chloe gave me a sympathetic look. "Anything I can do to help?"

"You're doing your part by keeping me from being buried alive in paperwork. Don't worry." I moved yet another stack aside. "All we can do is wait for an update from the police."

Much to my annoyance. I'd hoped to at least make use of my ability to speak to animals to find a witness or two, but either the creature itself or the person responsible had scared all the local wildlife away. Even from my office, I didn't see any birds outside the window at all.

"You're right." Chloe moved to rescue a stack of paper before it toppled to the floor. "I'll put all these files away. Anything else on your mind?"

"My inability to trust certain family members of mine not to call the press behind my back." I rubbed my temples, a headache brewing. "I'm guessing you saw the article in the *Blue Moon?*"

"I don't read tabloids." Her eyes widened. "No way. They already found out?"

"Thanks to my aunt, who must have called them right away." I scowled. "Or her daughter did, anyway. The article was written by the same reporters I forcibly removed from town, so they must have done the interview over the phone."

"I can arrange for someone to check they aren't staying in town." She returned her attention to her laptop and tapped on the keyboard. "Ah… I see what you mean. Clarice and Speck have some nerve putting their names on that interview."

"I know, right?" I'd banned the two reporters from town myself and had zero intention of giving them an inch, but it was kind of difficult for me to order them to leave me alone without getting in contact with them. "I'm not sure if the person who called them was behind the attack or just ready to take advantage of the impact on my reputation, but I'm not wasting my time by calling them myself."

"Not even to set the record straight?"

"Most of what they printed was true." Unfortunately.

"Yes, but they aren't going to stop with a single inter-view," Chloe said. "If I were you, I'd give them another warning, as well as the person who called them."

"They shouldn't be my priority. Besides, I already talked to my aunt, and I'm ninety percent sure it's her handiwork. Or her daughter's." My mind drifted to Rowan. She had Clarice and Speck's contact details from her previous interview, but she couldn't have been responsible this time. No, my aunt must have obtained their phone number herself. "I need to speak to Rowan first, in case she doesn't know what her mother might be up to."

"If you're sure." Chloe's mouth turned down at the corners as she scrolled to the bottom of the article's page. "You can drop by the café on your lunch break. I'll let your mother know where you are."

"Thanks." Mum wouldn't be thrilled at me for leaving the building right before the meeting, but it was that or run off when I was supposed to be filing paperwork. I doubted she'd slept a wink last night, so I could do without getting on her bad side. Instead, I kept an eye on the clock while I worked.

At lunchtime, I made for the door out of my office, ignoring Carmilla's pointed look in my direction. After successfully leaving the building without Mum waylaying me, I speed-walked down the high street. The winding street and its cosy shops showed no signs of the turmoil that had struck the forest the previous night, and the werewolf-owned coffee shop, Were's My Coffee?, was as bustling as ever.

I fired off a message to Rowan, letting her know I was outside. My youngest cousin now lived in a small flat above the café and worked there full-time, and aside from the occasional clash with Aunt Shannon's magpie familiar, she'd seen little of her family members since she'd escaped their house.

My phone buzzed with Rowan's reply, and I went to meet her at the back door. Her bright-pink hair stuck up in all directions, while her baggy T-shirt and leggings suggested she'd been gaming. "How'd you guess it was my day off?"

"I didn't." I followed her through the back door to the staircase that led to her flat. "This is the only chance I've had to escape the office in two days."

Rowan shot me a grin over her shoulder. "And you chose to come and see me and not Harvey. I'm flattered."

A pang of guilt hit me for not messaging Harvey since the previous night, but he already knew I'd be rushed off my feet tending to my guests all week. "We had a date the night I came back to town. Anyway, I thought you'd want to know that your mother is up to her old tricks again."

She halted at the top of the stairs, one hand resting on the wall. "Hold on, you think *she* set that monster loose in the forest?"

"You heard, then." I followed her into her flat, and she closed the door behind us. "I'm not sure if she did, but she's had all week to plot the best way to disrupt the meeting with the Head Witches, and what's more disruptive than a mysterious beast roaming around the Wildwood? The fact that the victim of the attack was a member of the Henbane Coven is another strike against her."

Rowan swore under her breath. "I didn't know a

Henbane witch was killed, but I guess it can't be Tiffany's work this time around."

"I thought not, but she's acting weirdly too." I shook my head. "She blames the shifters for some bizarre reason. Anyway, your mother is refusing to admit to anything, but I reckon she's the one who called the press. Did you see the names on the article in the *Blue Moon*?"

Rowan paled. "I swear I didn't talk to them, Robin."

"I don't think you did," I reassured her. "I think your mother or sister is behind that one, and they must have moved fast to have that story ready to go first thing this morning. Have you seen either of our reporter friends lately?"

"Definitely not." She pulled a face. "They don't need to be in town to fish for gossip though. Scumbags."

"No, but someone in Wildwood Heath must have spoken to them," I said. "Though I can't say I know why Aunt Shannon would have tipped off the press if she also brought the creature here. That's why I'm not sure it was her."

"Yeah, I don't see her setting anything loose in the woods," said Rowan. "Don't get me wrong, I know exactly what she's like, which is why I've been watching her the whole time you've been gone. Or Ralph has."

Her tarantula familiar, Ralph, poked out a leg from her sleeve. I smiled down at him. "Good idea. Did you see her going into the Wildwood at all?"

"Yes," Ralph said shyly, "but I didn't see any monsters. Have you asked the birds?"

"The creature scared them off," I said. "I've been trying to find any witnesses to speak to, but it's as if all the wildlife left that area of the woods altogether. That's one reason I thought someone with influence over the animals might have brought the creature here."

"I see your point," said Rowan. "I'll read the article and see if I can detect my mother's handiwork."

"Or your sister's," I added. "I bet she had Vanessa make the actual call."

"Good point," said Rowan. "I'll message you if I find anything. I take it you're stuck in meetings all afternoon?"

"Unfortunately, yes." I debated checking in at the police station on my way back, but that would draw unnecessary attention. I needed to have some actual evidence in hand before I accused anyone directly.

Especially if any of our guests turned out to be involved.

6

To no surprise, Mum was waiting to ambush me upon my return to the witches' headquarters, even though I'd left more than half an hour to prepare for the meeting. I crammed the last of the sandwich I'd bought on my way back into my mouth and chewed before entering the building.

"Where were you?" Mum eyed me while I sheepishly brushed crumbs off my cloak.

"I was getting some air before the meeting," I responded. "Don't worry, I didn't go near the forest."

"That wasn't what concerned me," Mum said. "Be careful with my sister."

She knew I'd spoken to my aunt then. "Noted. I didn't have time to check in with Ramsey, but I assume there haven't been any new developments overnight."

"Unfortunately not," she replied. "As of yet, the police haven't identified the creature, and neither have they found its hiding place."

"Or found any clues tracing it back to whoever set it loose, I take it," I added. "I wonder if any wildlife is ready to talk yet? I'd volunteer to speak to them, but I have prior obligations."

"Yes, you do," Mum said, again to no surprise. "Ramsey hasn't the time to scour the forest for witnesses who actually saw the creature. Given the level of disturbance the attack caused, it wouldn't surprise me if there weren't any."

Convenient. Like Mum, Ramsey didn't make use of his talent most of the time. He preferred using logic and intelligence instead of magic, and while talking to witnesses was a major part of his job, animals that weren't familiars didn't count. Granted, the local pigeons hadn't been much help, according to Tansy, but I refused to believe no wildlife had stuck around after the attack. They couldn't have left the Wildwood altogether, surely.

"I think it's worth looking into." I moved towards my office door. "Anything else?"

"Yes." Mum's lips pursed. "Today's meeting isn't set to cover the incident in the forest, and I think it's wise to stick to the agreed schedule."

"Assuming nobody else brings up the monster-shaped elephant in the room." When Mum gave me a stern look, I dropped the subject. "I should also mention that Mavis Willow was in front of my office earlier this morning. She seemed to be fishing for updates on the investigation, but Aunt Shannon said she's an expert on magical creatures. Is that true?"

"Yes, it is, but we'll discuss her later." She checked the time. "No deviating from the schedule."

"I assume I'm allowed to go and check in with Ramsey after the meeting is over?"

"Yes, I intend to do exactly that myself."

Good. "All right."

I entered the meeting room ahead of her to wait for the other Head Witches to arrive. At least this second meeting wouldn't begin with quite as many unnecessary and long-winded introductions as the previous one. Part of me had expected Aunt Shannon to skip out on the meeting, but like the previous day, she and Vanessa arrived last and sat at the far end of the table.

My patience frayed with every minute that passed. Isadora, dressed as ostentatiously as ever, spoke over anyone who wasn't a Head Witch and generally acted like a drama queen. Acacia took every opportunity to undercut her, while the rest of us barely got a word in edgeways. I cast the occasional glance at Mavis, wondering if she was genuinely willing to use her knowledge of magical beasts to help me or if Aunt Shannon had been baiting me. If I accepted her help, she might easily steer us in the wrong direction or take credit for finding the creature. As cynical as those thoughts might be, I really didn't know Mavis well at all, so I resolved to hold my tongue on the matter and hoped my brother would be able to identify the creature instead.

As for Aunt Shannon, she didn't offer any comments of her own, but her gaze flickered towards me upon occasion. Vanessa was glued to her mother's side like a limpet as usual, taking notes or possibly writing another report to hand over to the press. With Chloe as my notetaker, I tuned out Isadora's blathering and let my thoughts wander until Mum gave me a poke in the ankle with her foot.

"Ah, the last part of the meeting is open for questions. If anyone has any other queries they wish to raise, then now is the time to do so."

Please don't mention the monster. Please don't mention the—

To my bewilderment, Mum cleared her throat before anyone else could speak and addressed the other Head Witches. "If I may ask you all a question, when did you last consult the Seeing Stone?"

The Seeing Stone. The words sank into my mind, and I gave myself a mental shake for utterly forgetting the other reason we'd chosen to invite the other Head Witches to Wildwood Heath. Namely, the Seeing Stone—a magical item owned by each regional witches' council which functioned as a powerfully advanced kind of crystal ball and enabled anyone to peer into the future without the need to consult a Seer.

In the stories I'd read of past Head Witches, Seeing Stones were commonly used whenever a Head Witch sought certainty before making a decision. I could have used a little certainty in my life, but my real aim was to find out why I'd been chosen as a Head Witch. A Seeing Stone might be able to shed a little light on the reasons… if I found out who in this room currently held it. Each region's Stone was traditionally passed between the Head Witches every few weeks, and it hadn't been present in Wildwood Heath in years. From the silence that passed among the other Head Witches, I gathered that nobody wanted to admit to experiencing any doubts.

Mavis spoke first. "The last time I consulted the Seeing

Stone was with regard to a delicate situation with the local vampires, but the answers it gave were too vague to apply. Viewing the future is an inexact art, even for Seers, after all."

From her phrasing, I couldn't tell if she'd meant to imply that she carried the Seeing Stone herself. According to Grandma, the Stones belonged to the council as a collective but were passed among its members so that each person had a chance to use the Stone when they needed to. My own time might take a while to come around, given how new I was to the job, but that didn't mean I couldn't borrow it from its current owner.

Yes, I might have visited a Seer instead, but Seeing was one of the rarest types of magical talent, and most Seers could only see glimpses of the future at most. The Seeing Stone was unique in that any witch could use it, not just people gifted with the ability to see into the future.

"Inexact is an understatement," Acacia said. "I believe the last time I consulted the Seeing Stone was more than a decade ago, and its answer was decidedly murky."

"That I don't doubt," Jemima said. "The Stone is more of a guide and a tool than an accurate predictor of real events."

Acacia gave a false laugh. "No Head Witch with any sense would rely upon a Seeing Stone even as a guide."

That figured. I hoped *she* didn't have the Stone, though Mavis and Jemima exchanged raised eyebrows at their fellow Head Witch's assessment.

"Seeing Stones might not be a hundred percent reliable, but they have their place," Mavis said. "Yes, one might see a dozen possible outcomes and not know which will come to pass, but in some cases, it's better than walking into an uncertain future."

"The future is uncertain by definition," said Acacia. "Is it not?"

Isadora made a disparaging noise. "We have no reason to fear the future, not if we carry on as we always have and don't give in to pressures to change our ways."

"A worthy statement, to be sure." Acacia's words dripped with so much sarcasm it was a wonder the room didn't flood. "There are always incidents that disturb the peace, however, and it's somehow necessary to adapt if we want to ensure they don't destabilise everything we have built over the past few decades."

Her gaze flickered to me briefly. *I'm a disturber of the peace, am I?* Possibly true, but I didn't appreciate the implication that I'd somehow decided to disrupt the usual state of affairs by getting myself chosen as Head Witch. No Seeing Stone had warned anyone of *that*. Knowing Acacia, though, she was readying herself to bring the topic around to the paranormal hunters again and how they were the only solution for dealing with these so-called disturbances.

I cleared my throat. "The future is uncertain, true, but a sceptre picks the next Head Witch, not a Seeing Stone."

Another fake laugh came from Acacia. "The sceptres we wield are no more sentient than a Seeing Stone, and they certainly have no influence on *my* decisions. You, of course, might feel differently."

Had she forgotten that if not for the arbitrary judgement of a sceptre, none of us would be sitting in this room? Maybe she hadn't faced any real challenges on her own path to becoming Head Witch, but she must have thought a lot of herself to believe her position infallible.

Mum shot me a warning look, but I refused to let the slight go unchallenged. "Interesting. If the sceptre isn't sentient, then that would suggest that chance alone determines who becomes Head Witch."

"Don't be absurd," Acacia responded. "It isn't chance that directs the sceptre's choices but the will of the goddess—that is, the will of magic itself. The sceptres might be mere tools, but they are placed in our hands by the goddess because we are the best positioned people to wield them."

I stifled a sceptical snort. I didn't give much thought as to whether an all-powerful goddess of magic actually existed, but believing she was goddess-chosen made the term "egotistical" look like an understatement. "Does that include the numerous Head Witches in the past who turned against the councils or gave up their positions?"

Acacia shifted in her seat but maintained her haughty expression. "In certain cases, the goddess's choices might be limited. When a Head Witch dies suddenly, for instance."

I had to admire her nerve in taking a swipe at my entire family. Fury flickered through Mum's expression, though she kept her outward reaction under tight control, while Aunt Shannon's brief smirk vanished when the implication sank in that she hadn't been worthy of being chosen in the eyes of the goddess either.

"That's all very well," Mavis interjected, "but I think some of us might want to keep our attention focused on more immediate issues."

She wasn't wrong. I needed to find out why I'd been

chosen as Head Witch, undoubtedly, but finding the culprit behind the attack in the forest should be my short-term priority. Whatever had placed the sceptre in my hand, be it fate or luck or the goddess herself, I needed to use whatever resources I had at my disposal to find the source of the attacks. Including the Seeing Stone.

"Agreed," Mum said. "I think we should wrap the meeting up for today, don't you? Assuming nobody else has any questions."

Nobody did. While the others began to leave the room, I lingered behind, intending to find out if Mavis did indeed have the Seeing Stone in her possession. As if she knew I wanted to talk to her, Mavis dawdled on her way to the door. When the two of us were among the last handful of witches in the room, I followed her outside.

"Mavis," I began. "Do you have the Seeing Stone? Did you bring it with you?"

She gave me an assessing look. "Yes, it's currently in my room at the inn. Did you want to use it to find the source of the attack in your forest?"

Was I that easy to read? At least I'd confirmed she held the Seeing Stone and not one of the others, but their comments on the unreliability of seeing into the future had cast doubt on the notion of using it to solve any of my current problems.

"I might," I replied. "I haven't spoken to the police today yet though, so I'd prefer to do that first."

"A wise idea," she said. "It must be tricky to solve a crime with no obvious suspects."

She'd guessed the attack hadn't been random. It wasn't hard for an outsider to reach that conclusion, but I couldn't help wondering if she'd seen the article. Even the Head Witches had access to the Wizarding Web.

"The police have dealt with worse." I kept my tone neutral. "We'll solve this, I'm sure."

"I don't doubt you will." She lowered her voice. "The level of attention on your town can't make it any easier to deal with."

"Attention?" I echoed. "Wildwood Heath is a tourist spot. We're used to hosting events such as this one."

"Yes, I suppose you're right," she said. "I didn't mean to overstep, but I wanted to make it clear that I don't condone anything my fellow Head Witches might have said."

She overtook me to catch up to the other Head Witches, who'd already left the building, while I wondered what she'd meant to imply. Maybe she was just trying to offer support. Whatever the case, if I wanted to find out who the killer was, following my mother's instructions to avoid mentioning the subject to the other Head Witches wouldn't do any good… but she hadn't said I couldn't discuss the attack *outside* of the meeting room.

After leaving the witches' headquarters, I called my familiar to my side. Tansy came sprinting over from the back garden at once.

"Have fun today?" I asked.

"Not really." Tansy scaled my leg and climbed up to her usual spot on my shoulder. "There's still barely a blackbird in sight, and I got bored looking for action in the Henbane Coven's garden. I think Tiffany has gone back to the police station to pester your brother."

"Oh great." I would rather have avoided *her* if I could help it, but before I checked in with Ramsey, I thought I might as well direct a few pointed questions at certain other Head Witches. Meaning Acacia. She deserved to be taken down a peg for her jabs at me in the meeting, and for all I knew, her belief in her goddess-given power held a more sinister undertone. Of all the Head Witches, she seemed to dislike me the most, which was a good enough reason to place her on my list of suspects for the monster's presence in the woods.

I quickened my pace, surreptitiously, catching up to Acacia. When she tilted her head to acknowledge me, I attempted a polite tone. "I hope you're enjoying your stay here. Are your accommodations to your liking?"

She sniffed. "They suffice for a town as small as this one."

"Good." I ignored the slight, doubting that she'd come from a community that was any bigger than ours. "I hope the rest of the week is equally pleasant for you."

"Indeed, despite the unfortunate circumstances." The note of mockery in her delicate tone prepared me for what would follow. "The attack in the forest must have been a great inconvenience for you."

"Rather worse for the victim."

"Naturally," she said. "The article in the *Blue Moon* this morning speculated on whether the attack was linked to the presence of visitors in town."

My heart skipped a beat. She read the *Blue Moon*? She hadn't been the one who'd contacted them, had she? With difficulty, I affected a nonchalant tone of feigned surprise. "I wouldn't expect anyone of your status to read our tabloids. They're considered tacky and sensational by most."

"Ah, but they do contain useful information sometimes, don't they?" She smiled. "In fact, they often tell truths that others would rather be kept quiet."

"That would depend on where they get their information." Might as well have it all out in the open. "Some tell the truth, but a larger number are happy to twist the facts to their own ends, and that particular tabloid is notorious for crossing boundaries in pursuit of an agenda."

"Then I suppose it depends if the subject of the press's mockery has influence enough to keep them from crossing those boundaries, wouldn't you say?"

The cheek of it. "Even my grandmother wasn't immune to their persistence. Her tried-and-true strategy was to ignore them, the same way I do."

Her mocking expression faded. "Yes, she was a wise woman. A tragic loss was hers, both to your town and to the magical world itself."

She actually liked my grandmother? That might explain her dislike of me, but she might as easily be lying through her teeth. For a brief moment, I debated telling her Grandma's ghost was alive and kicking, relatively speaking, but that would have gone against Grandma's own commands.

"Agreed," I said instead. "On the subject of the press, I'm more concerned about the impact of the rumours on the victims of the attack."

"Well, of course," she said. "I hope the case is resolved before the week's end."

"As do I." Wait, how many more days would they be in town? Two? Despite the endless hours in meeting rooms, the week was flying by faster than I'd anticipated. "You'll be heading straight home at the end of the week?"

"Yes, with the Seeing Stone."

"The—Seeing Stone?" I stopped in my tracks. "I thought Mavis Willow had it."

"It changes hands, don't you know?" Her smile was back. "I expect your turn will come… eventually."

She walked away while I watched with a growing sense of dread. If I didn't borrow the Seeing Stone from Mavis soon, Acacia would take it first, and I was willing to bet she wouldn't loan it to me without a price.

As I approached the police station, mildly rattled from my talk with Acacia, my phone buzzed with a message from Rowan. *My sister called them.*

I stared at the message in confusion before remembering Rowan's offer to do some sleuthing to find out who'd been responsible for the interview with the press. That was the easy bit though. Finding out who'd actually committed the crime was another matter entirely.

Pocketing my phone, I walked into the police station through the automatic doors, where Ramsey's office door lay open on my left-hand side. I heard both his voice and Mum's conversing behind the door, but they stopped talking when I entered the office.

My brother looked even more tired than he had the previous evening, as if the entirety of the stress he'd missed on our week away had fallen on his shoulders at once. "I thought you had work to do."

"Nice to see you too," I said. "Did the medical reports come back?"

"Keep it down." He glowered at me until I closed the door behind me. "Yes, and Tiffany's not thrilled. The results are inconclusive."

"What do you mean, inconclusive?"

"The wounds on the victim don't appear to have been inflicted by any animals known to live in the Wildwood," he said. "Whatever attacked that girl isn't in the records of any creature we have on file."

Tansy shivered on my shoulder, while I shook my head. "That can't be right. I know we don't often run into manticores in the woods, but we must have them in the records. I mean, what if one of them escapes from a zoo?"

"Manticores aren't kept in zoos, Robin."

"I'm aware of that, Ramsey. It was an example."

"If a manticore did get loose in the area, then a team of experts would be sent in to recapture it," Mum put in. "If not, then one of us would need to call in a specialist."

"If we don't know what we're actually up against, would a specialist be able to help?" I asked.

"In all likelihood, yes," said Ramsey. "But that would involve exposing our dilemma to an outside party."

"You did see the *Blue Moon*'s headline this morning, didn't you? Everyone knows already." I tried to catch Mum's eye, but her attention was on my brother, and I had no doubt her thoughts were in alignment with his.

"Yes, the tabloids know about the attack," Mum said, "but they don't need to know that we're unaware of the cause."

"Then what do you want to do?" I let Tansy climb down my arm so she could jump onto the desk. "I assume you aren't volunteering to hunt down the creature yourselves. Given everything else we have going on, it'd be a challenge even if we did know what we were up against."

"We won't be in the dark forever." Ramsey irritably moved a stack of papers aside before Tansy knocked them off the desk. "I have my team spread throughout the forest, looking for more clues as to the nature of this beast. I hoped the medical report might help, but so far, the injuries don't match any of the better-known magical beasts."

A shiver sprang to my arms. "Have you spoken to any of the wildlife yet? They had a front-row seat to the attack."

"No, they didn't," said Prickles, who sat atop a filing cabinet. "Besides, most wild animals aren't capable of intelligent thought."

"Ooh." Tansy flicked her tail at him. "Did another pigeon crap on your head?"

"That's enough." Ramsey shooed Tansy off his desk. "Most of the birds who've flown into town in the past day came from elsewhere, so they didn't witness the attack in the forest. It wouldn't surprise me if every animal in the immediate area fled the scene and won't be back for weeks."

"And that doesn't worry you?" Tansy climbed back onto my shoulder, her little voice indignant. "I've never seen the forest so quiet in all my life."

"Tansy would know," I added. "Also, we can't rule out that the person who did this intended to make the wildlife steer clear precisely so that you wouldn't have anyone to question. It'd be hard to pull off without our family's gift but not impossible."

"You don't need to tell *me* that," Ramsey said. "There's such a thing as a coincidence, Robin, and the arrival of any dangerous predator in the forest would be likely to scare off the wildlife regardless of how it got there."

"If the person responsible arranged for the attack to take place right behind our houses, then it's not unfeasible for them to have engineered the wildlife's response too," I pointed out. "Whether or not they actually used a gift like our family's."

Mum exhaled. "Robin, I told you my sister didn't do this."

"She did talk to the press," I said. "According to Rowan, it was probably Vanessa who did the actual interview, but we know who put her up to it."

"Of course we do," Ramsey said, his expression disgruntled. "It makes sense for the pair of them to take advantage of our situation, but that doesn't change anything."

"Doesn't it bother you that Aunt Shannon is watching our every move with the intention of reporting our failings to the press?" I asked. "To Clarice and Speck, to be precise. You know, the journalists I kicked out of town weeks ago."

"Wasn't Rowan the last person who spoke to them?" Ramsey asked.

"She isn't involved this time." Of that I was certain. "But Aunt Shannon was certainly quick on the mark."

"That doesn't mean she was responsible herself," Mum said firmly. "Regardless, it's clear to me that we never should have gone away so soon before the summit."

To my irritation, Ramsey nodded in agreement. "Precisely."

"Wasn't it your idea?" I addressed Mum. "If we'd stayed at home, Aunt Shannon would have come up with a different plan instead. Unless we'd had a Seeing Stone, we'd never have predicted this."

"A Seeing Stone." Ramsey's gaze slid to Mum. "Who has it, do you know?"

"Mavis Willow," I answered. "Might it be able to help us identify the creature? She only has it until Friday, but if I ask nicely, she might loan it to us."

"Absolutely not," Mum cut in. "Besides, the Seeing Stone has its limits."

"Didn't you plan to have me consult the Stone myself at the first opportunity?" I asked. "Also, Acacia Bracken is going to take it next, and I'd rather not ask *her* to loan it to me. She thinks it's a waste of time."

Mum's jaw twitched. "If the Stone goes to her next, then we're better off waiting until later. We aren't in a hurry."

"*You* might not be." So much for Mum wholeheartedly supporting my commitment to finding out why I'd been chosen as Head Witch. "If I have to wait, I might as well talk to a Seer instead."

"A Seer isn't going to help us find this creature," Ramsey said. "We need to see the present, not the future. The beast seems to have either moved deeper into the woods or otherwise hidden itself from sight."

"Typical." Not surprising, given that the town was surrounded by woodland on all sides. "Has anyone on your team tried flying above the forest on a broomstick?"

"Have they tried what?" Ramsey looked askance at me. "No. The trees would mask the creature from sight."

"Just a thought."

Raised voices reached my ears, cutting through my brother's reply, and I recognised one of them as Tiffany Henbane's.

"I'll deal with this." Ramsey walked to the office door and pushed it open.

On the other side, a dishevelled Tiffany glowered at us. "Well? Have you found the attacker yet?"

"The police are doing their best," I told her. "If you let them do their jobs, then they'll be quicker to find answers."

"They haven't spoken to a single shifter."

Not this again. "That's because a shifter didn't attack Rachel."

"I *saw* the medical reports," she spat. "Rachel was mutilated by a clawed beast. How can it have avoided detection if not by hiding among humans?"

"The monster scared off all the other wildlife in the surrounding forest, Tiffany," I said. "If shifters were capable of that, there'd be nothing living in the Wildwood at all."

"Exactly," Tansy piped up. "You tell her, Robin."

Tiffany's eyes narrowed. "You'll regret this. All of you."

She turned on her heel and left the building. Ramsey watched the doors close behind her without a word and then returned to his office.

"Well, that was instructive." I joined him, as did my mother. "What's with her sudden fixation on shifters?"

"I haven't the faintest idea," Ramsey said irritably. "Perhaps they're a convenient target to blame, given that they live near the forest."

"She's never liked that the shifters aren't bound to follow the covens' laws," Mum said. "I assume it's her way of reconciling with the knowledge that nobody in her coven will be Head Witch. She has to feel superior somehow, so she's set herself against other paranormals instead."

"That figures," I said. "She accused our coven of conspiring against her to avoid finding answers. Never mind that we're here trying to solve the murder of one of her coven members while she walks around making ridiculous accusations."

"She feels threatened," said Ramsey. "Someone in her coven was attacked, after all. I'm trying to give her the benefit of the doubt."

"She doesn't make it easy," I said. "But she has a point in that the creature has managed to avoid detection for a while. Not that it has any shortage of places to hide. She's seen the medical reports, right?"

"Yes, and the wounds aren't dissimilar to those inflicted by an enraged werewolf," Ramsey acknowledged. "We know they weren't because shifters leave traces. Fur, footprints… they're not subtle. They also don't attack anyone unless they're directly threatened. Tiffany ought to know this, but she ignored everything I told her."

I grimaced. "It's just like her to use this as a chance to air her grievances, but do either of you think she might be overcompensating to divert suspicion from her own coven?"

"No… even she wouldn't go as far as to attack her own coven members," said Mum. "That said, we can't discount the possibility that the person behind the attack is local."

"I thought that was a given." I frowned. "Unless it was one of our visitors, but if anyone among our guests is on the suspect list, they'll have to be questioned in the next two days. They're all leaving town at the end of the week."

"Not an option," Mum said. "That Acacia Bracken is a nasty piece of work, make no mistake, but I doubt she's behind this."

"I'd like to see her knocked off her pedestal at least," I said. "Though if she hears a word about Tiffany's theories on the shifters, she'll start banging on about those paranormal hunters again."

"She what?" Ramsey's gaze sharpened. "The paranormal hunters?"

"She thinks we ought to increase their presence in the region," Mum said. "There's no chance the others will agree to it."

"The hunters are specialists," Ramsey said. "They'd certainly be able to deal with this monster."

"You can't be saying you agree with her?" I asked incredulously. "For all we know, she set this situation up herself in order to get her way."

Most people in Wildwood Heath would object to the paranormal hunters moving in even on a temporary basis. They tended to act on their own instincts when it came to hunting down rogue paranormals, and they didn't necessarily care about the laws of the paranormals whose territory they trampled all over in the process. The shifters would get the brunt of the backlash if the hunters started swarming around the forest in pursuit of monsters, and the coven would deal with the public impact. None of it was worth the risk.

"I doubt she did," Mum said. "Don't mention anything of the sort at tomorrow's meeting, Robin."

"I don't have a death wish." Though I wished anyone

but Acacia was next in line to take the Seeing Stone. "Right… I'm going home."

"You mean to the forest," Ramsey corrected.

"You're welcome to come with me."

There was no reason why not, in fact. Ramsey might not make active use of his talent most of the time or even use magic at all, but he'd been top of every class at the academy, and some of our teachers had been disappointed when he'd exiled himself from the coven's formal duties rather than attempting to buck tradition and serve on the council. In fairness, he was good at his job and was the youngest police captain in the town's history, but if he'd followed in Mum's footsteps, that would have all but guaranteed I wouldn't have been chosen as Head Witch.

Then again, without me being there, it might well have been Aunt Shannon who'd claimed the sceptre instead. I'd have needed a Seeing Stone to make sense of all the options. Though considering Grandma *had* had access to a Seeing Stone and hadn't seen any of this coming, it was no wonder the other Head Witches were sceptical of them at best.

Ramsey ignored my suggestion entirely. "I'll continue to look at our files on magical beasts. Try not to get in my team's way, will you?"

"As if." I turned to Mum. "I'm trying to help, you know. I'll see you later."

I left before she could snag me in another lecture on the dangers of the forest. On my way out of the police station, my phone started buzzing in my pocket. I checked and found an unknown number calling me.

I weighed the odds then answered. "Hello, who is this?"

"Robin Wildwood, it's so good to speak to you again!" said an indistinct feminine voice. "This is Clarice from the *Blue Moon*. Remember me?"

Seriously? "Yes. I distinctly recall telling you never to show your face here again."

I could hardly believe she had the nerve to call me on my personal mobile phone. How had she even got my number?

"We got off to a shaky start the last time we met, didn't we?" From the way her voice buzzed, she was calling from a remote place with little phone reception. Like, say, a forest. Oh boy. "I would like it very much if you would give me a second chance to interview you. We can do it over the phone if you prefer."

"Like my cousin Vanessa, right?"

"Exactly."

My free hand clenched. "What do you want with me, Clarice? You think I'll happily dish the dirt on my own family?"

"Not at all. We simply want the Head Witch's perspective on the current events in Wildwood Heath."

"I can give you that for free," I said. "My perspective is that if you set foot in Wildwood Heath again, I'll have you arrested."

"That isn't necessary." She sounded wounded. "I'm sorry I overstepped your personal boundaries last time we spoke, but I'm happy to let you speak for yourself."

"Or twist every word I say, I'm sure." She couldn't possibly think I'd backtrack at this point. "As a matter of fact, I'm busy with meeting with the other regional Head Witches for the rest of the week. I'm sure my cousin can give you more than enough material to work with."

I ended the call, then I blocked her number for good measure.

Tansy's fluffy tail tickled my ear. "You're going to have to get a new phone number, aren't you?"

I groaned. "Depends how she found out. And if she shared it with anyone else."

I was willing to bet the answer to the first point was "Vanessa" and the second was "everyone," but I had zero intention of wasting the rest of the daylight hours faffing around with phone numbers when I had more pertinent issues demanding my attention. Namely, the reason the press had called me to begin with.

Tansy jumped off my shoulder and scampered ahead of me. "You probably shouldn't have taunted her about asking Vanessa for material."

"She'd have done it anyway. I just hope she isn't hassling Rowan as well."

I could almost have guaranteed she'd try, but I trusted Rowan not to give her the time of day. Still, I texted her a warning so she'd have a heads-up if they called her and then made for the Wildwood.

8

To avoid sparking an argument with Ramsey's colleagues, I opted to enter the Wildwood via one of the paths over on the western edge of town, not far from my dad's cottage. I realised I should probably pay him a visit at some point, though he'd no doubt heard about the attack by now. He wouldn't be pleased if I mentioned Tiffany's accusations towards the shifters, but I would hope she'd have the sense to avoid a direct confrontation with the local werewolf pack. Most likely, she'd keep hounding my brother instead.

Upon entering the forest, I scanned the leaf-strewn path and the low-hanging branches in search of any wildlife. Then I whispered a general command directed at any animals within hearing distance.

Tansy's ears pricked, but there came no response. "They won't hear you. Not unless you shout, and then you're more likely to attract Ramsey's officers than anyone else."

"True." I'd need to go farther afield, and while I carried the sceptre, that didn't mean I couldn't be taken unawares.

I kept an eye on the treetops as I walked, repeating my command every so often, but the branches remained eerily silent. The quiet set my nerves on edge, and I didn't blame Tansy for running back to my side. Perching on my shoulder, she peered ahead of us. "Are you going to visit your dad?"

"Might as well now that I'm in the area."

Upon reaching his cottage, I rapped on the door. Dad answered after a short pause, beaming at me.

"Robin!" He gave me a one-armed hug to avoid knocking the sceptre out of my hands. "I thought you'd be busy all week."

"I am… but I thought I should talk to you about the incident in the forest the other day. I figured you would have heard the news."

"I heard." His smile faded. "A girl was attacked, right?"

"A witch. From the Henbane Coven." Behind him, I heard the boisterous sound of Jessica's kids playing in the living room and lowered my voice so they didn't overhear. "The police haven't figured out what attacked her yet, but we're guessing there's some kind of wild beast in the area."

"The police don't know what attacked her?" His forehead creased. "Strange."

"There's no tracks," I explained. "Or any other signs to point to its identity. It's also scared off all the wildlife in the area, so I can't even question the birds or squirrels."

"I thought it was a bit quiet out there," he said. "Jessica went for a run earlier, and she said she's never seen the Wildwood so silent."

"Yeah… I'd stay indoors for the time being," I advised him. "Make sure you tell Jessica and the kids to avoid the woods too."

"Of course," he said. "I suppose this is another thing you have to deal with as Head Witch. Anything I can do to help?"

"The local shifters didn't see anything, did they?" I asked. "Or hear anything odd around the time of the attack? No witnesses have come forwards yet, but I can't believe nobody else was outside."

His brow crinkled. "Strange. I don't know anyone who did, but everyone is taking the police's orders to stay out of the woods seriously. We're taking the kids to the park instead."

"Good call," I said. "You'd think the werewolves' leader would object to a wild beast encroaching on his territory."

"It's not really the pack's territory," he commented. "In fact, the entire Wildwood technically belongs to your coven."

"True." No doubt the reason it'd been targeted in the first place. The shifters might prefer to live near the forest, but I didn't believe any of them had been involved. Tiffany's irrational rants had nothing to do with reality. Regardless, if this was really Aunt Shannon's doing, she'd taken a major gamble with the town's safety if she'd left the beast to roam the woods unchecked.

Dad glanced behind him. "I need to step in before someone knocks over that giant LEGO model. See you soon?"

"Of course." I took a step back. "I should head home before it gets dark."

"Stay safe," he called after me.

Back on the woodland path, I followed the route towards the site of the attack. Tansy regained her nerve and scaled the occasional tree to scout ahead of us.

"If we keep going that way, we'll run into the police." She indicated the path with her tail. "There's nothing here except a few insects. They're no help."

"Figures." Insects weren't exempt from my abilities, but they had a tendency to speak far too fast for me to understand a word they said. "You know, I shouldn't waste my time searching on foot. I need a bird's-eye view, even if there aren't any actual birds around to speak of."

"You mentioned looking down from the sky," Tansy commented. "I don't see Ramsey dusting off his old broomstick, but you can give it a shot, can't you?"

"My broom's at home." Though thanks to the incident a couple of weeks ago when I'd had to catch an escaped criminal in flight, I knew how to use the sceptre to cast a conjuring spell. Unlike a wand, the sceptre required no preparation even for the most complex spell.

Raising the sceptre, I pictured my broomstick in my mind's eye. A flash of light followed, and my broomstick landed in front of me. "Let nobody say I don't use my powers for good."

"Handy," Tansy remarked. "I'm surprised you don't use that spell more often."

"I don't need to make it a habit." With the way the sceptre amplified my usual magical abilities, it was often tempting, but I knew better than to become reliant on an instrument that I owned on a conditional basis. The sceptre might have chosen me as Head Witch, but I didn't believe for a minute that we were as closely bound as a regular witch and her wand.

Besides, unlike certain other Head Witches, I didn't for a minute believe I'd been chosen by any goddess nor that I was somehow superior to the alternatives available at the time. The other Head Witches had held positions of power in their covens *before* being chosen, whereas I'd been pushed to the fringes of mine when I hadn't lived up to expectations. Not remotely comparable. I didn't even *want* the sceptre to take up permanent residence in my home.

Mounting the broom, I took flight more carefully than usual to avoid crashing into the low-hanging tree branches. As we ascended, Tansy hid herself inside my sleeve to keep from being showered with leaves.

I wasn't as accomplished a flier as Harvey, but I steered us through the canopy without any accidents and slowed to a sedate pace while I scanned the treetops for any signs of life. Several birds wheeled around the sky but too far from the forest for me to catch.

I was on the tail of a group of seagulls when a loud *crack* from the trees below startled me so much that I nearly fell off the broom.

"Something's going on down there!" Tansy exclaimed.

I gripped the broom with my free hand and scanned the forest in search of the source. My gaze caught on a patch of trees, where two trunks leaned against each other at odd angles, and a scream came from somewhere below.

I descended, raising the sceptre, but I didn't dare cast a spell without making sure there wasn't anyone in the way. *That scream... it belonged to a human.*

Branches scraped my arms with the speed of my descent, but I hardly noticed. My attention was fixed on the lopsided trees, but I saw no signs of whatever had knocked them over. That scream though—

My stomach plummeted. Nearby, Mavis lay sprawled on the path, bleeding from several deep cuts. Her sceptre was clutched in her hand, a trail of smoke swirling around the end. Her own spell must have hit the trees instead of her target, but where had it gone?

My feet touched down next to her, and I hopped off my broom and raised the sceptre. Light bloomed at the end, casting a purple glow over the trees.

"Come out and face me," I warned the forest at large. "Too cowardly, are you?"

Tansy tugged at my sleeve. "You have to get her out of here."

"I know, but I can't carry her on my own." I raised the sceptre again. "Hey! Anyone out there?"

A blast of light shot up from the sceptre like a beacon, dazzlingly bright. Oops. At least I was confident that everyone in the vicinity would have seen me, but there wasn't so much as a branch out of place aside from the two fallen trees Mavis had knocked over while defending herself.

Where on earth was her attacker? I hadn't seen anything from the sky, so it must still be on the ground somewhere—but where?

Rustling sounded in the bushes. I tensed, then Mavis's familiar poked her head out of the leaves and croaked in despair. "Mavis!"

"Did you see what attacked her?" I asked. "I've called for backup, but I can't carry her by myself."

"No." Helena hopped towards me. "She told me to hide, and I did. I'm a terrible familiar."

"You aren't." I crouched. "If her sceptre didn't hurt that creature, then she'd have wanted you to hide rather than risk your life. Come with me and Tansy. I'll get you out of here."

The toad hopped onto my outstretched hand. Keeping hold of the sceptre with two familiars balancing on my free arm was tricky, but I cast a spell to send my broomstick back home so I wouldn't forget it in the forest. Then I fired off another beacon, certain the police officers patrolling the forest couldn't be far away.

Sure enough, within minutes, two officers came jogging into view. Both let out exclamations at the sight of Mavis's fallen body.

"I found her like this." I held up her familiar, who croaked in agreement. "I don't know where her attacker went."

"Where were you?" One officer examined Mavis's body while the other called for backup. "Did you see what attacked her?"

"No—I was on my broom. I saw a disturbance from the sky."

I did a double take when none other than my mother showed up with two more officers.

Mum's eyes widened at the sight of Mavis—and me. "What is this?"

"She was attacked," I explained, raising my voice so the newcomers could hear me. "I was on my broom at the time, watching the forest from above, when I saw a disturbance down here. I found her like this. I think she knocked the trees over in self-defence."

Mum sucked in a breath. "This is going to cause problems."

"You don't say." I'd missed the creature by seconds, surely, yet it'd vanished as if into thin air. The lack of any animals in the area only cemented my certainty that the creature was no ordinary monster.

While two officers carted Mavis off to hospital, I let Mum steer me away from the scene.

"When did she come into the woods?" she asked. "She must have slipped past the officers watching the paths."

So had I, but I knew the forest inside and out. Mavis didn't. "I spoke to her after the meeting, but that was a while ago. Maybe she came here to do some investigating of her own."

Had she figured out what the creature might be? Until she regained consciousness, we wouldn't be any the wiser as to what had attacked her, but she'd be lucky to survive. Rachel hadn't, after all.

The town's hospital was located on one of the many roads branching off the high street. Mum headed for the Owl's Nest Inn to inform Mavis's fellow coven members of the attack, while I waited awkwardly outside the hospital, not wanting to use my Head Witch authority to push the staff into letting me in when Mavis was unconscious and couldn't talk anyway. It was safe to say my plan to ask her to borrow the Seeing Stone had crashed and burned, but that was the least of our problems. For one, the rest of her coven would find themselves in a sticky spot if she didn't recover. Her sceptre... wait, how had her sceptre not been able to help her defend herself against her attacker? Nothing about her fate made sense.

Questions bounced around my skull as I waited. When Mum returned with Mavis's coven members in tow, I handed Helena to one of them and then snagged Mum's arm before she could follow them into the hospital. "Mum, I need to talk to you—"

"Later, Robin," she said. "I'm sure Mavis will be able to give us a full report of the attack when she wakes up."

"Are you sure she will?" I lowered my voice when one of the witches nearby gave me a dirty look. "Who has her sceptre?"

"She's in good hands." Mum began to walk away. "As for the sceptre, her coven has it, and I have no doubt they have contingency plans in place no matter the outcome."

I hastened to catch up with her. "Do you think Aunt Shannon knows yet?"

"No, I imagine she's at home."

"And you're sure she isn't wandering around the woods as well?" I glanced over my shoulder. "Should we check on the others at the inn? There's no telling who else might have got it into their heads to do some private investigating while our backs were turned."

"I did check," she said. "All the other Head Witches are present, and I doubt anyone else will take it upon themselves to venture into the forest."

Good. Yet the attack had taken place deep enough inside the woods that the creature must have known Mavis's location. Either it'd tracked her by scent or something similar… or someone had set it upon her.

The question was, why? Because Mavis had been close to finding out the creature's identity? Possibly, but there was also the chance that the creature had acted like any predator would upon finding human prey in its vicinity. The real question was, how had it vanished so fast?

I drew in a breath. "Mavis is supposedly an expert in

magical creatures. I think she went looking for it herself and got taken by surprise."

"Do you now?" Mum asked. "You think it was an accident?"

"Personally? Not a chance." I shook my head. "I don't know if she thought she could track the creature herself or if she just got curious, but she was definitely looking for it when it found her."

"I doubt anyone else will get the same idea."

"That's not what worries me." A shiver ran down my spine. "I was on my broomstick right above the forest when it attacked her. I landed moments after the attack, yet I didn't see any signs of the creature at all."

"Be glad you didn't."

"I think you're missing the point." I kept my voice quiet. "It's like the creature vanished into thin air. It certainly didn't fly away, so either it ran faster than any beast of that size has the right to, or it turned invisible. Do any of those options sound likely to you?"

"Robin, I understand why you're worried, but it's the police who have to find the creature, not us," Mum said. "If it's in the area, I have no doubt Ramsey's team will find it before nightfall."

No. I had an inkling the creature was long gone, while learning the truth hinged on Mavis's recovery from the attack.

If even a Head Witch hadn't been able to fight off the monster, though, did the rest of us stand a chance?

9

With my plan to search the forest myself dead and buried, I ended up in Rowan's flat. Mum had reluctantly given me permission to go out as long as I didn't try tracking the creature myself, but I knew better than to think I'd be able to find our elusive monster with the police and half the coven swarming all over the woods.

Equally unlikely were my chances of talking to Mavis, who remained unconscious but stable, according to the hospital staff.

"I can't believe the beast attacked a Head Witch," Rowan said when I'd finished telling her. "That's messed up."

"I can't figure out how it vanished." I watched from the sofa while Tansy amused herself by peering into the tanks and cages in which Rowan kept her spider collection. "I was hovering directly above the forest when it attacked Mavis, but it was gone by the time I landed. How's that even possible?"

"Is she likely to survive?"

I grimaced. "They put her odds at fifty-fifty, but it depends if the creature's wounds have other nasty side effects like poison. Rachel didn't make it, after all."

"Was she one of the Head Witches who didn't like you?"

"Nope, I think she was trying to help me." Guilt jabbed at me again. "She knew all about magical creatures, but I was too suspicious to ask for her advice."

"Was that why she went out alone then?" Rowan gave a low whistle. "It's lucky you found her when you did."

"Wish I'd got there sooner." I rested my head against the back of the sofa. "I swear I should have landed right on top of that creature. It shouldn't have got away."

"You might be the one in hospital if it hadn't," Rowan murmured.

Fair point. "At least if I'd fought back, I wouldn't be the one to take the fall if she dies."

She raised a brow. "Is that what the other Head Witches said?"

"I haven't spoken to them since the attack." I slumped against the cushions. "Mum checked nobody else had wandered off and then left the inn before they started asking too many questions. There's no way she can keep the details quiet though... and I don't even know what we're going to say at tomorrow's meeting. If there is one."

"This can't be the first time a Head Witch has got injured on the job, can it?"

"No, but it's certainly *my* first time handling anything like this." I ought to ask Grandma if she'd ever had a similar experience, but I had zero desire to go near the office again today.

"No kidding." She exhaled. "You can't be faulted for not knowing Mavis would try to track the creature alone."

"I'm sure the press will find a way to blame me anyway."

"Yeah… Vanessa's fingerprints are all over that interview." Rowan pursed her lips. "I don't think she set that monster loose though. Nor my mother. Sure, they're capable of it, but risking the life of another Head Witch is way over the line."

"True, but I'm all out of other theories," I said. "Including on what kind of creature it is, for that matter. Has Ralph noticed anything weird going on with the local wildlife?"

"Nah, but we're right in the middle of the town, as far from the forest as you can get," she said. "Tansy hasn't coaxed any of the pigeons into answering questions?"

"Nope." My gaze went to Tansy again, who was currently engaged in a staring contest with one of Rowan's tarantulas. Considering the spider had rather more eyes than Tansy did, I figured she was in a losing battle, but it kept her occupied. "Tiffany Henbane thinks a shifter did it."

The recent attack wouldn't disprove her theory either. A shifter could certainly have attacked someone and then turned into a human again, therefore seeming to vanish—but that was only one explanation and not the most plausible one by far.

Rowan blinked at me. "I thought she'd accuse you first."

"Oh, she's definitely keen to tell me how I've mishandled the situation." I pulled a face. "She also accused me *and* the police of being prejudiced against her coven."

"Maybe she attacked her own coven member and is going to extreme lengths to divert suspicion."

"That wouldn't be out of character, I admit, but would even she launch an attack on a Head Witch?" My phone buzzed in my pocket. "This better not be Clarice and Speck again."

"Please tell me you told them to shove it."

"In more polite terms, yes."

"They have some nerve." A flush lit her cheeks. "For the record, they haven't called me, but if they do, I'll hang up."

"I know. Let's see who's messaging me." I pulled out my phone and found a message from Harvey asking if I was free that evening.

"Not the press, given the look on your face." Rowan gave a sly smile. "At least I *hope* it's not them."

"Definitely not. It's Harvey."

"Going to see him?" She tilted her head to one side. "Your mother told you to avoid the forest, didn't she? She didn't tell you to avoid the pub."

"True." My family would be less than thrilled at me for going on a date when the coven was in a crisis, but the Fox's Den was as far from the forest as it was possible to get. "You know what, it's entirely worth risking their wrath."

A date with Harvey would be a nice bit of sanity, and if anything, I'd be less likely to argue with my family members if I kept out of their hair.

Rowan grinned. "That's what I like to hear."

Ten minutes later, I sat opposite Harvey at a table in our favourite local pub, having finished relating the utter mess of the past week.

"The good news is that my mother has thrown the idea of me pretending to be a competent Head Witch twenty-four, seven out of the window," I finished. "So here I am. I don't *exactly* have permission to be here, but she ordered me to stay away from the forest, and I'm honouring my word."

It didn't entirely sit well with me that I was in a cosy pub with my boyfriend rather than helping the police search the forest, but my own skills were of limited use in this situation. I did best when I had a clear target, and the mysterious beast in the woods was the exact opposite of clear.

"It doesn't sound as if anyone should be wandering around the forest," said Harvey. "Have the police figured out what kind of creature it is yet?"

"Apparently a creature that can either turn invisible or move at the speed of light." I poked at my meal with a fork. "Mavis can't tell us anything until she wakes up, and her familiar didn't see the creature. The poor thing was hiding in the bushes to avoid being caught in its path."

"Why was Mavis wandering around that deep in the woods, anyway?" he queried.

"I *think* she was looking for the creature, but it's anyone's guess as to whether she actually knew what it was." I put down my fork. "I screwed up. She all but offered me help, and I turned her down because I knew my family would raise a fuss."

"You didn't screw up." He reached out and took my hand across the table. "Any creature that can take a Head Witch by surprise isn't likely to be easy to find."

"I wish that helped." I gave a humourless laugh. "The worst part is that the other Head Witches—except one—

are the *last* people I'd ask for help with anything. Now my one potential ally is in the hospital."

He gave my hand a squeeze. "If you like, I can fly above the trees and have a look around. That's about all I can do to help. Sorry."

"Honestly, just you being here with me is enough." I managed a small smile. "Everything's gone to hell at work, my coven is in disarray... even the forest isn't safe. This is the only place I can find any sanity, except for Rowan's flat."

"She's okay then?" he asked. "I saw that article in the *Blue Moon*... and I recognised the names."

"Rowan didn't talk to them this time, but her sister was all too happy to dish the dirt." I picked up my fork again. "My aunt too. I don't know if they were involved in the attacks as well, but my mother flat-out refuses to entertain the possibility of her sister being responsible. Regardless, tomorrow's meeting is going to be a joy."

"You're still meeting up with the other Head Witches?" he asked. "Can't you... I don't know, postpone the meeting? You have a good reason to."

"Not sure the other Head Witches will see it that way." Granted, one member fighting for her life might be enough of an excuse to put the more mundane issues on hold. "I'll see what Mum says."

My mother's reactions were a tad unpredictable at the moment, but I didn't blame her, given the current mountain of pressures on our family.

"I'm sure this counts as an emergency situation," said Harvey. "The other Head Witches would understand, I'm sure."

"Some of them would," I acknowledged. "I can think of

one who definitely wouldn't, and as luck would have it, she's the one who's next to take the Seeing Stone from Mavis."

"Seeing Stone?" he echoed.

"A magical artefact that belongs to the regional witch council," I explained. "In the interests of fairness, it changes hands between Head Witches every few weeks, and it's supposed to be with Mavis until she hands it to Acacia at the end of the week. It enables anyone who holds it to see into the future."

"No kidding?" His brow furrowed. "Wait, did you want to use the Stone yourself?"

"Am I that obvious?" I smiled weakly. "Yes, I did. For several reasons, though this mysterious monster wasn't originally one of them. Acacia… I don't see her agreeing that Mavis being in hospital is enough of an excuse not to follow convention, so she'll probably snag the Stone at the first opportunity."

"And you don't want her to know that you need to use it," he guessed. "Is it likely to be able to help you find the person responsible for the creature in the woods?"

"At this point? Who knows?" I sighed. "I hoped to at least identify it, but the local wildlife seems to have fled the area. I searched the forest myself before the attack."

His brows shot up. "You do realise that sceptre of yours doesn't make you invincible, don't you? Please don't risk your life."

"I won't."

I just wanted to know what we were dealing with… aside from "trouble," which went without saying. Trouble for the coven, for the town—and for my future as Head Witch.

———

The following morning, I checked the news before I even got dressed so I'd be forewarned if any new stories were floating around. The *Blue Moon*'s headline woke me up more effectively than a caffeine shot: *Head Witch brutally struck down: is the Wildwood Coven responsible for releasing dangerous predator?*

"You have got to be kidding me." Anger blurred the words before my eyes, and I blinked a couple of times to get my focus back.

Reports say the woman was attacked by a vicious beast that fled immediately into the forest after wounding her. According to witnesses, Head Witch Robin Wildwood found her body but was unable to find the creature.

"Witnesses?" I muttered. "A likely story."

The identity of the creature has even the wisest of Head Witches stumped, but there may be a simpler explanation at hand. The beast appeared to vanish into thin air, but it may have simply taken to the skies to make its escape.

"Let's ignore the fact that I was on a broomstick at the time, then." Evidently these "witnesses" had overlooked that part.

Then I saw the next line: *Reportedly, the current Head Witch and the leader of the Wildwood Coven were involved in an incident involving an infant dragon and its parents recently in which they helped the family relocate away from human habitation. Perhaps their act of kindness resulted in terrible consequences.*

I let out a loud curse that might have been heard from the other side of the Wildwood and put down my phone, seething. Taking in a deep breath, I threw clothes on as fast as I could, snatched up the sceptre, and ran downstairs.

I found Mum waiting for me in the living room, having presumably heard my outburst. "What is it this time?"

"You haven't seen the news?" I waved the phone in front of her nose. "The *Blue Moon*'s mysterious consultant has decided that the dragons we helped relocate are behind the attacks."

Her lips compressed. "I have to admit that I thought they'd bring that up sooner."

"You guessed?" I said disbelievingly. "This is absurd. The dragon can't have followed us all the way here. I know they can fly, but I was on a broomstick at the time anyway. If they'd asked actual witnesses, they'd know."

To add insult to injury, the reporters had risked causing harm to an innocent group of creatures in their quest to undermine me. *Aunt Shannon has gone too far this time.*

"The journalists might have tried to call you if you hadn't scared them off."

"So now it's my fault?" Mum had reacted to my date with Harvey yesterday with little more than resigned exasperation, so I'd hoped that we'd be on the same page with how we proceeded with the investigation. Apparently not. "You know they'd have gone straight to their first contact, who happens to be my cousin. Nothing I said would have made a difference to how they wanted to spin their story."

"Precisely," Mum said. "Put it out of mind. Don't forget you have another meeting in two hours."

"Didn't I already tell you I wanted to postpone?" She

had to be joking. Who could focus on a meeting at a time like this?

"You'd run the risk of the press assuming you don't take your job seriously."

I gave a brittle laugh. "Yeah, and if I go ahead, they'll say I'm callous and uncaring for disregarding an injured Head Witch. There's no winning. How'd they even find out about the dragon? You didn't tell anyone but Jemima, did you?"

"No, but they're experts at finding information."

"And printing lies." Maybe Jemima had told the press about our adventure without necessarily knowing what they'd do with that information, but it was just as likely that my aunt had found out through her own sleuthing.

In fact, if I confronted Aunt Shannon and her daughter head-on, they might not even deny responsibility. They knew they hadn't technically broken the law and that anything I did in retaliation would only make me look worse. Besides, what kind of retaliation would even work on my aunt? I had more power and influence than she did, and yet she'd still managed to undercut me.

Worse, she shouldn't even be my priority. The person who'd set that monster loose in the woods ought to be my primary target, but with Mavis hospitalised, my chances of identifying the creature had shrunk to almost nothing.

"It's up to you if you want to postpone," Mum said. "You're the one who'll make the final call."

"Right." The sound of birdsong drifted through the kitchen from the back window. By the looks of things, my outburst of anger had attracted a few pigeons, and Tansy was happily chasing them around the garden. "I'll be back in a second."

Hoping the wildlife would be more helpful today, I ran outside and made for the bird feeder. "Tansy, slow down. Don't scare everyone off."

"They're pigeons." She leapt forwards and pinned down a stray feather. "They don't know anything."

"Hey," I called to the nearest pigeon. "Have you been in the forest lately?"

"No!" The pigeon flapped its wings, agitated. "The forest is wrong."

"Wrong?" I echoed.

"Wrong!" chorused the surrounding birds, taking flight in a shower of feathers.

"Hey!" I reached out with my free hand, but their feathery wings slipped through my grasp. "Can't one of you be a little more specific?"

"What *are* you doing?" Piper emerged from behind a flowerbed. "Talking to the birds?"

I dropped my hand. "I hoped one of them saw our invisible monster."

She blinked. "If it's invisible, they wouldn't have seen it, would they? Wait, is it *actually* invisible?"

"That makes more sense than the alternatives." I picked a feather out of my hair. "I was flying directly above the forest where it attacked Mavis. By the time I landed, her attacker might as well have evaporated on the spot."

Her eyes widened. "Did it use a transporter spell?"

"Only a witch or wizard can use a wand." That didn't mean someone else hadn't used a spell *on* the creature, of course. "Vampires are fast, but they don't have claws."

"Shifters do. Some of them, anyway."

I winced. "Don't say that so loudly. Tiffany thinks it's a

shifter, but it's based on an irrational dislike of them and nothing more. Besides, can you imagine a shifter doing that to a person?"

"A rogue might, but otherwise, no." She shook her head. "I was just throwing out ideas. If your elusive monster is that good at avoiding attention, then it must be easily as intelligent as a human."

"Unlike those birds," said Tansy. "The pigeons are useless."

"What did they mean by 'wrong'?" I asked. "They were talking about the forest, right, but what's supposed to be wrong? Did they mean the creature isn't supposed to be there?"

My gaze followed the pigeons' retreat over Aunt Shannon's garden. Familiars were generally more intelligent than the average wild animal, but the only bird familiars who might have flown above the woods this morning were Myrtle the magpie and Hector, Vanessa's sparrow familiar. Neither of them counted as a reliable witness.

Piper followed my gaze. "Think your aunt knows something?"

"I'm a hundred percent sure she does. Have you seen the headline story in the *Blue Moon* today?"

"No, because I prefer not to look at drivel first thing in the morning."

"Not a bad idea, but those journalists have gone too far." Behind me, I saw Mum beckoning me into the house. "Check it out. Fair warning—it's grim."

I left Piper to her rosebushes and returned to Mum's side. "What is it?"

"The other Head Witches have been making plans to

leave immediately after the meeting," she said. "That is, today."

"Seriously?" A day ago, I'd have been more than happy to wash my hands of them all, but if another Head Witch had been behind the attacks, letting them walk free was out of the question. To say nothing of how they'd leave with the worst possible impression of our town *and* our coven.

"Yes, so you'd better be quick to come to a decision."

Pressure much? "Right, then the meeting will be postponed. It's either that or name the other Head Witches as suspects and call them to the police station for questioning, and I don't think they'd appreciate that much."

"Postponing isn't a permanent solution either," Mum warned. "Some might already have prior engagements."

"We'll risk it," I said. "I can delay until the end of the week. I just hope Mavis will wake up before then."

10

"What do you mean, postponed?" Acacia scowled at me across the lobby of the Owl's Nest Inn. "Until when?"

"Until Mavis wakes up," I replied. "If she doesn't recover before Friday afternoon, we'll hold the meeting then and you can depart. Most of you will only leave a day later than the original plan."

"I have a hair appointment," Isadora said from near the stairs. "On Friday morning."

"I'm sure the world won't end if you reschedule." Oops. I probably should have reined in the sarcasm a little. "I'd prefer for everyone to be present at the meeting, including Mavis. It's only fair."

"That's all very well, but the rest of us have plans that can't be delayed," said Isadora. "Is the meeting really that urgent?"

You tell me. I hardly cared for the meeting at all, but I should have guessed she and Acacia would act as if I'd suggested that we should relocate our final meeting to the moon.

"I think we should vote on it," Isadora said. "Where is Jemima?"

"In her room, I assumed." With both Isadora and Acacia in the reception area of the inn along with several of their fellow coven members, I was already outnumbered, but I'd volunteered to break the bad news to them. It would ruin the impression that I had the situation under control if I brought my mother with me. "I think hosting the meeting without Mavis would be unfair."

"What if she doesn't wake up?" Acacia asked. "What then?"

"The staff at the hospital are doing everything they can to help Mavis." Jemima walked into the lobby to join the others. "I think Robin is right. It doesn't seem appropriate to proceed with the meeting with the spectre of this creature hanging over us."

Spectre. An accurate enough description of our monster—and if I didn't know that most spirits couldn't even touch people, let alone inflict mortal injuries, I might wonder if it was a ghost after all.

Acacia made a disgruntled noise. "We should ask the rest of the council their opinions in the interests of fairness. I wonder if the other members of the Wildwood Coven would agree."

"They're busy helping the police. My whole family is." Not quite the truth, since Aunt Shannon hadn't volunteered to help out and neither had her older daughter, but the thought of my aunt walking blithely around and enjoying the chaos grated on my nerves.

The rest of the coven had left the police to handle it,

though I didn't blame them, considering the creature had nearly killed a Head Witch the previous day. Mavis was stable, according to the hospital staff, but she hadn't woken up yet. Nor had anyone brought up the Seeing Stone, but I knew it wouldn't be far from Acacia's thoughts. She'd have to take the Stone regardless of whether Mavis survived.

Isadora looked at me with interest. "Has the creature been sighted yet? Or has it attacked anyone else?"

She sounded far too enthusiastic about that possibility for my liking. "Not that we're aware of, no, but the police are working around the clock."

Judging by the fact that my brother hadn't come back the previous night, I figured that was the accurate truth.

"Doesn't your coven *own* the forest?" Acacia queried. "If it were mine, I'd be calling for backup. The paranormal hunters would certainly be able to handle a case like this."

Oh boy. I should have figured that she'd find another way to bring the subject straight back to the hunters. "Given that another witch is likely responsible for the creature's presence here, then it's not appropriate to hand over the investigation to the hunters."

She arched a brow. "Another witch?"

Ack. I'd spoken without thinking, but it was too late to take back my words. Now, all three Head Witches focused their attention on me, and none more so than Acacia.

"So that's what everyone is trying to keep secret." She gave a nod as if satisfied with herself for guessing. "You think another witch is responsible."

Oops. Yet having the truth out there might be exactly what I needed. "The creature near-fatally wounded a Head Witch. It's safe to say that it's either far more dangerous than the average magical beast, or it has the aid of another person."

"Do dragons typically team up with witches?" asked Isadora.

Of course she'd seen that article. "No, and a dragon wouldn't have been capable of the damage that creature did. Besides, they can fly. I was on a broomstick over the forest at the time of the attack, and if the monster had taken flight, I would have seen."

"You were on a broomstick?" Acacia didn't look convinced, but Isadora was nodding as if I'd confirmed a theory of hers.

"Yes, I thought that it would be easier to track the creature from the sky," I told them. "I wasn't aware that Mavis had ventured into the forest alone. Were any of you?"

The last time I'd seen Mavis before finding her in the forest, she'd been heading back to the inn with the others. Someone must have seen her slip away.

"No," Jemima replied. "I heard her leave the inn, but I assumed she went to run an errand. I'm surprised the police didn't see her enter the forest."

"She didn't use any of the main paths." I studied the other two witches, trying to read their expressions. Isadora was a closed book, as usual, while Acacia projected her typical disdain. "In fact, I wonder if she knew the monster's location. Did she mention if she had any theories?"

I figured not, but I was curious to know if Mavis had discussed the subject with the others at all.

"No, but surely your police will find whatever trail she

was following," Acacia said. "If they're as dedicated as you claim, at any rate."

"They are, but I would prefer for this to be resolved as quickly as possible." Major understatement. "If you know anything concerning Mavis's presence in the woods that might aid the investigation, then I'd be grateful if you told me."

"I do not," Isadora answered.

"And nor do I," Acacia said. "Would the police like us to offer our assistance as well?"

"If we're going to stay here for the duration, we might as well do something useful," Isadora put in. "I'm sure the Head Witch will reward those who help her."

Why had they chosen *now* to start agreeing with one another? "With respect, Mavis tried to help and was attacked. I would prefer the same not happen to anyone else."

"*Was* she trying to help, I wonder?" Isadora queried. "Or was she acting alone?"

"Until she recovers, we can only speculate." Jemima came to my rescue. "However, I'm sure Robin and her coven wish to handle this alone."

"We do," I confirmed. "I intend to help the police myself while I wait for Mavis to recover."

"Do you now?" Acacia asked. "What if the creature attacks you too?"

She has some nerve. "That won't happen."

"I remember hearing a similar statement from your predecessor," said Acacia. "We can never truly predict our fates, can we?"

"My grandmother was murdered," I said through clenched teeth. "I was chosen to replace her as Head

Witch in part because I caught her killer, and I would thank you to be a little more respectful."

I'd probably given too much away, but Acacia had some nerve attacking my grandmother when she'd been a better witch than everyone else in this room put together.

"Precisely," said Jemima. "If there *is* a human perpetrator, then I have no doubt that Robin has the skills to find her."

"I agree." Isadora jumped to my defence, to my surprise—though maybe I shouldn't have been, given her general dislike of Acacia. "As for me, I *suppose* I can rearrange my hair appointment, and I will inform my coven that I'll be staying in Wildwood Heath for another day."

Well, well. If I'd known that mentioning my grandmother would be the fastest way to gain the others' cooperation, I'd have done so sooner.

"As will I," said Jemima.

"See that you do the same," I told Acacia. "If you have any complaints, then please direct them to my assistant."

I hoped they wouldn't, for Chloe's sake if nothing else. Since I'd placated the other Head Witches for now, I left the inn, looking around for my familiar.

Jemima followed me outside. "Do you really intend to track the creature alone?"

"Not alone, no." I spoke in a low voice. "But I'd prefer that nobody else steps into harm's way, particularly my guests."

"Isadora and Acacia might not go into the forest, but they'll certainly tell their covens of the reasons for the meeting being rescheduled. Fair warning."

"I didn't think they'd appreciate my other idea." When

she gave me a questioning look, I added, "Ordering them to go to the police station to be questioned on their potential involvement in an attack on a fellow Head Witch."

She sucked in a breath. "*Do* you think one of them is involved?"

"No, but there are only so many reasons I can think of to delay the meeting that won't fall outside of the regulations. You'd think the near death of their fellow Head Witch would be enough, but apparently not."

"You aren't wrong," Jemima said. "I'd be glad to offer my help if you need it."

"I'll let you know if I do."

Before that, though, I intended to pin down Aunt Shannon.

While Jemima returned to the inn, I spied Tansy lurking in a doorway next to a large green toad. Mavis's familiar.

"There you are." I strode over to them. "Helena, what are you doing out here?"

"I can't stand another moment in that hospital," she croaked tremulously. "And I won't listen to those other witches gloating at the inn."

"Are they now?" I debated heading back in and telling them to cut it out, but I'd already given them enough of my time. Unless one of them was behind this after all, I was better off searching the forest instead.

Tansy scampered over to me. "Do you think she knew?"

"Do I think who knew what?" I asked blankly.

"Do you think Mavis knew what that creature was before she went looking for it?"

"Ask Helena, not me." I turned my attention to the toad, who shrank back. "I thought you said she didn't tell you anything."

"She didn't," the toad confirmed. "If she knew, she didn't say a word to me."

"I can go and sneak a look in her luggage," offered Tansy. "See if she left any clues in there."

"What?" Helena sounded scandalised. "You can't do that."

"If she'd been carrying any evidence with her, the police would have already found it," Tansy said. "If she left it in her room though? That's a different story."

"Good point," I said. "Helena, I know you want to protect your witch, but we want to find out what that creature is before it can attack anyone else."

Even if she hadn't said a word to anyone else, she might have written down her theories on the creature. If magical monsters were a fascination of hers, she might even have brought a textbook that went more in depth on the subject than any of our own resources. You never knew.

"I'll be back soon." Tansy ran back towards the inn and scaled the drainpipe, while I turned to an indignant Helena.

"Don't leave me here!" she wailed.

"What do you want me to do, bring you back to my office?" I asked. "Or return you to Mavis's hotel room?"

"Take me with you."

Oh boy. "If you turn out to be conspiring behind our backs, I'll leave you out to dry."

"Never," she croaked. "How could you say such a thing?"

"It's happened before." She looked so pathetic sitting there that I felt sorry for her, and if she kept hopping around unsupervised, she might end up being snatched up by one of the local seagulls. "Right, fine, come with me."

I scooped the toad up in my non-sceptre hand and then carried her down the high street. I'd have to ask Chloe to watch her while I went to talk to my aunt—both to inform her of the postponed meeting and to ask a few pointed questions about her involvement in the second attack. I assumed someone had already told her the details, but my conversation with Piper earlier had reminded me that one explanation for the creature's mysterious disappearance was that someone else had been present. Someone who carried a wand... and who knew the Wildwood inside out.

Upon reaching the Wildwood Coven's headquarters, I made for my office and dropped Helena onto a bemused Chloe's desk. "What... who's this?"

"This is Mavis's familiar," I told her. "She doesn't want to be alone while her witch is in hospital, and I think she'll be safer here than hopping around town."

As long as Carmilla didn't wake up and try to eat her, anyway.

"I'll watch her then," Chloe offered. "Did you speak to the other Head Witches?"

"I did. I've told them the meeting is postponed until Mavis wakes up, and now I need to do the same for the council."

"Want me to help?"

I shook my head. "It's no bother. Can't be worse than telling the other Head Witches."

After leaving the office, I climbed the stairs straight to

the upper floor. When I found Aunt Shannon's office locked, I rapped on the door anyway, but she didn't answer. Undeterred, I proceeded to seek out all the other council members and inform them of the postponement, but none of them knew whereabouts Aunt Shannon had gone.

Rattled, I returned to my office and found Grandma's ghost floating next to my desk.

"There you are," said Grandma. "I thought you were supposed to be meeting with the other Head Witches today."

"We postponed the meeting so nobody can sneak off before we find the person behind the attacks," I said. "Instead, that seems to be exactly what Aunt Shannon has done."

"Has she now?" Grandma scoffed. "Trust her to take advantage of everyone's distraction and sneak out."

"That or she wants to avoid me." I faced my assistant. "Did you see the nonsense the *Blue Moon* printed today?"

"I saw." Chloe's hands tensed on the desk. "It's terrible. I wish there was something I could do to stop them from printing those lies."

"You asked the other Head Witches to stay in town?" Grandma didn't appear particularly concerned about the press's antics. "I thought you'd be clamouring to get rid of them."

"I am, but I have several reasons for asking them to stay," I replied. "One of which is that Mavis currently has the Seeing Stone, but it's due to pass to Acacia at the end of the week."

"You're hoping she wakes up so you can borrow it?" Grandma asked.

"It's not my top priority, but I'd rather arm-wrestle that monster in the forest than ask Acacia to lend it to me. This might be my last shot to get my hands on the Stone before she slithers off with it."

"Oh, her." Grandma gave a short laugh. "Acacia has always been unpleasant to deal with."

"She seemed to like you, but she also insulted us both at least once," I told her. "Though… you've met her and the others dozens of times, haven't you? Does anyone among their group strike you as likely to have been responsible for unleashing a monstrous creature in the forest?"

"You think one of *them* is responsible?" she asked. "Didn't you and your mother meet up with Jemima for a friendly chat the other day?"

"I meant Isadora and Acacia," I clarified. "Mavis is currently fighting for her life in hospital, and Mum seems to trust Jemima more than the others, but you personally knew all of them. You'd know if Isadora or Acacia was capable of anything like that, wouldn't you?"

"Oh, they're capable, but Isadora would be more likely to challenge you directly to your face," she said. "Acacia is too cowardly. She has a sharp tongue, but she's afraid of retaliation."

"She insulted us, did she?" Carmilla lifted her head. "What did you say in response?"

"I told her to be more respectful," I replied. "I also reminded them that I solved the former Head Witch's murder."

If a ghost was capable of blushing, my grandmother would have turned bright red. "You did what? You dared to use my death as a ploy to get them to stay?"

Ah. I should have guessed she'd take it badly, and I immediately regretted saying anything at all. "Is it better than them knowing your death was an accident and not murder? I didn't know how else to convince them, considering Isadora was convinced her hair appointment was more important than the meeting."

"You are absurd."

The sound of the front door opening outside my office made me spin on my heel. *Aunt Shannon.* "Back in a second."

I sprinted out of the office, nearly colliding with Aunt Shannon on the other side of the door. The sceptre slid from my grasp, but I caught it between my fingertips at the last second. That was a close one.

"Head Witch." Aunt Shannon looked down her nose at me. "Why the rush?"

I didn't even bother faking a polite smile. "I want to inform you that today's meeting has been postponed while Mavis recovers from her injuries."

"How kind of you," she said. "Were the other Head Witches amenable?"

"Of course." I heard Grandma's voice from behind my office door, possibly complaining to Chloe or her familiar, and a surge of recklessness seized me. "You know, Aunt Shannon, I've given you the benefit of the doubt up until now, since you're obviously suffering from a fit of jealousy over losing your title, but endangering lives is a step too far."

"Endangering lives?" She laughed. "Whose life have I endangered? Yours?"

"The dragons', of course," I said. "I suppose it didn't take too much effort for you to find out what Mum and

Ramsey and I were doing on our way back from Ivory Beach, but that doesn't mean you needed to risk the paranormal hunters going after the dragons we helped to relocate simply because you wanted to make us look too incompetent to manage the Wildwood."

"Dragons?" she repeated. "That's what you were dealing with?"

"Obviously." Had she thought feigning ignorance would work on me? "I know you were watching our every move, no doubt with Clarice and Speck on the other end of the phone."

She gave me a withering look. "I have better things to do with my time. Especially this week, given that we have a killer in town. A killer of Head Witches, no less."

"You had Vanessa do the last interview. Don't deny it."

"You're wasting both my time and yours," said Aunt Shannon. "I rather think this particular story has Tiffany Henbane's fingerprints all over it."

"What do you mean, Tiffany?" I asked. "One of her coven members *died*. She's been hassling the police for the past few days, and she thinks that a shifter is behind the attacks. She didn't have time to call the press."

"I was under the impression that she wanted you out of power, no matter who else got hurt in the process."

Is she being truthful? Tiffany *had* been surprisingly fierce in defending her dead coven member considering how little she'd seemed to care about her fellow witches in the past, but blaming the dragons didn't further her goals.

Or maybe it did if her intention was to have me removed as Head Witch.

Aunt Shannon swept past me. "If you don't mind, I'd like to return to my office."

She made for the stairs, leaving me rooted to the spot. *What in the world?* Either she'd upped her acting skills, or she genuinely hadn't been responsible for today's news story.

But if she hadn't spoken to Clarice and Speck and told them about the dragons, then who had?

11

I returned to my office to find Grandma's ghost had vanished. No doubt she'd gone into one of her sulks, but I hadn't the patience to go looking for my grandmother when she didn't want to be found. Not when Aunt Shannon's words had rattled me beyond belief.

Tiffany Henbane. Might Aunt Shannon be right? It'd be entirely in character for Tiffany to have intentionally tried to waste my brother's time with theories she didn't actually believe in herself. Had she gone as far as to arrange the death of one of her own coven members though?

My office door nudged inward. I tensed, but it was only Tansy, back from Mavis's hotel room. She hopped onto my desk, her fluffy red tail swishing. "No luck. The other Head Witches got into Mavis's room first."

"Seriously?" At Chloe's questioning look, I added, "Tansy went to check Mavis's room to see if she left any clues behind about the creature in the woods."

"You think she knew then?" Chloe eyed Helena, who sat on the desk as far from Carmilla as possible.

"She didn't tell me," Helena protested. "She wanted to keep me safe, so she ordered me to hide as soon as she heard the creature's approach."

"What did the attack sound like?" I asked. "Can you describe what you heard?"

The toad shuddered all over. "Growling… snarling. It was horrible."

That wasn't very specific, but the poor thing was traumatised enough without me making her relive the experience. I turned to Tansy instead. "Fancy spying on the Henbanes?"

"Why?" she asked.

"Aunt Shannon suggested it was Tiffany who told the press about our detour to relocate those dragons."

"She would say that," Tansy said. "She's willing to go to any lengths to divert blame from herself."

"She's a better actress than I gave her credit for then," I said. "She seemed to genuinely not know anything about the dragons, and I wouldn't be surprised if Clarice and Speck did try calling Tiffany. I can guarantee she'd jump at the chance to give them an interview."

"That she would," Tansy acknowledged, "but the article didn't mention the shifters, and Tiffany thinks they're to blame, doesn't she?"

"I don't think she does. Her main goal is to kick me out of my position by any means necessary."

"Obviously," said Tansy. "Tiffany though? You think she's more likely to have given the game away than your aunt is?"

"I don't even know." I sat down at my desk, weariness

coursing through me. "Both of them are trying to undermine me."

My office door opened again, and this time, Mum walked in. "Good, you're back at work."

"Thanks for knocking." I rubbed my temples. "Yes, I brought Mavis's familiar here. Chloe's keeping both eyes on her, don't worry."

Mum's gaze flickered to Helena. "What exactly did you say to the other Head Witches? My mother seems to think you've given them the impression that she was murdered by an assassin."

"Would you rather I'd been truthful?" I lifted my head. "They were on the verge of packing their bags and leaving. It was that or tell them to present themselves at the police station for questioning, and I don't think they'd have liked that very much, do you?"

"Robin." She exhaled in a sigh. "Why *is* Mavis's familiar here?"

"She didn't want to be left alone at the hospital or in the hotel room, so she was wandering around town," I explained. "I didn't want her running into trouble."

"Shouldn't that be hopping?" Tansy looked up at Mum. "Also, you might want to talk to your sister."

"Why, exactly?" Mum asked.

"She claimed she never knew about the incident with the dragons." I rolled my eyes. "She seems to think Tiffany spoke to the press instead."

"My sister didn't know," Mum said. "I made sure word didn't get out."

"She might have found out in the past couple of days. That familiar of hers is nosy enough." I rose to my feet.

"Whoever did the interview, we have a serious problem on our hands."

"Yes, we do." She peered out of the window with narrowed eyes. "Did you invite the other Head Witches here?"

"No, I most certainly did not."

"Well, they're here. All of them."

"What?" Alarmed, I glanced towards the window and spied a familiar group of cloaked individuals approaching the building. Oh no. "Jemima said she was willing to help me out, but I declined. I made it clear that I'd handle this myself."

"We need to keep them away from the forest," Mum said. "I suggest coming up with an excuse for another meeting."

"Meeting?" I echoed. "Over my dead body. I already told everyone else on the council that today's gathering was postponed. What are they even doing here?"

"They're bored," Tansy said. "They want you to entertain them."

"I'd ask them to help search the forest, but I won't have another attack on my watch." *Think, Robin.* "Should I send them to research obscure magical monsters?"

"Do you have enough books?" Tansy perched on a cabinet to peer out the window. "Looks like they brought the rest of their coven members with them too."

"Oh, for crying out loud." I jumped a foot in the air when someone rapped on my office door. Before I could begin to formulate an excuse to send them packing, Mum opened the door to reveal Jemima standing outside.

"I need to talk to you alone." To my consternation, Jemima addressed my mother, not me. "Urgently."

"Without the Head Witch?" Mum glanced at me. "Robin, find out what Isadora and the others want. I'm sure you can find a way to keep them entertained."

Oh, come on. But I couldn't send poor Chloe to order them around, not least because they might refuse to listen. Dread gripping me, I pushed open my office door a moment before Isadora came sailing into the lobby. Acacia followed, making a beeline for the meeting room.

"Might I ask what you're doing here?" I asked Isadora in as polite a tone as I could muster. "There's no meeting scheduled—"

"So this room is free, I assume." Isadora caught up to Acacia outside the meeting room. "It's more convenient for us to meet here than the lobby at the inn."

"For what reason?" What were they playing at?

The rest of the coven members entered in a pack, also swarming towards the meeting room, and I resignedly followed them in.

"I have a theory," Isadora announced. "I believe the person behind the attacks intended to undermine the authority of the Head Witches."

Huh? Where'd that come from? "What makes you say that?"

"Mavis worked out the truth about the creature," said Isadora. "That's why she was attacked."

"That I agree with." If we found common ground, it might be easier to move forward. "However, until she wakes up, we can only speculate on what she found."

"What if the creature targeted her precisely because of her status as Head Witch?" Isadora asked. "Nobody else has been attacked."

"The first victim wasn't a Head Witch." Now she'd lost

me. "The creature is either able to turn invisible or move faster than any known predator, or it's being commanded by a person with magical abilities. That's who we need to find."

"Yes, and the witch responsible doubtless hates everything we stand for," Isadora insisted. "It's not the creature we should be worried about but the person commanding it."

Well, true. If a witch was commanding the creature—Henbane or otherwise—then they might have cast a spell to hide the beast from sight or otherwise make us unable to track it down. And if it *wasn't* Aunt Shannon, the culprit might still be in the forest right this instant.

"Let me deal with the witch myself," I said. "The police are hunting down the monster, and I've no doubt the person who brought it here won't be far behind. They've ordered everyone to stay out of the forest so they can do their jobs."

"Yet you intend to help them without any information." A smirk appeared on Acacia's face. "Allow me to offer an alternative."

She reached into her bag, pulled out a large, glowing green stone, and put it down on the meeting room table. A hush permeated the room, and the breath fled my lungs. The glowing green stone reflected our own faces back at us, while my thoughts spun in circles. Mavis must have left the Stone in her hotel room while she'd been in the forest... and now Acacia had taken it for her own.

"I thought you didn't believe the Seeing Stone was of any use in making decisions," I commented. "Also, it's my understanding that one can only view the future, not the present, so using the Stone to find the creature's current location won't be possible."

"But it *can* reveal the person responsible." Her smirk grew more pronounced. "Right?"

Yes. It could, and it shouldn't have surprised me that she'd come to the same conclusion. If I'd known Mavis had the Seeing Stone with her sooner—if I'd accepted her help—then I wouldn't be facing this dilemma.

I said nothing, but Acacia's eyes gleamed with triumph as she leaned over the glass. "I will ask the glass to show me the potential outcomes of us investigating this killer."

Before anyone else could react, Acacia pressed the palms of her hands to the gleaming stone. Her entire body went still, her gaze fixed on the stone's rippling surface as if it were a window into another realm.

Curiosity seized me in spite of the overwhelming instinct to knock the Stone out of her hands. I cast a glance at Isadora, whose expression reflected the same desire to know what Acacia was seeing—but a moment later, Acacia released the Stone, and its glassy surface returned to its prior murkiness.

Anger glittered in her eyes. "The Stone is as cryptic as ever, I see."

It didn't work? "What did it show you?"

"I'm not obligated to tell any of you," Acacia said sourly. "But it's clear that our only option is to go into the forest and hunt down this creature ourselves."

"Excuse me?" I could still hardly believe Acacia had had the nerve to snatch the Stone from Mavis's possession while she was in hospital, but her plan was out of the question. "Mavis nearly died. Do you want to risk suffering the same fate?"

"We're Head Witches," Isadora said. "We shouldn't run in fear, whatever we're up against."

"There's running in fear and there's being reckless," I said. "I told you the police have the situation in hand. Besides, if you storm into the forest and raise a fuss on the town's doorstep, you run the risk of someone innocent being caught in the monster's path."

"We'll lure the creature into a trap then," Acacia said. "I'm sure your coven's headquarters contains something we can use as bait, as well as a net or a similar contraption."

Whatever had happened to Grandma's assertion that Acacia was too cowardly to act? Worse, our coven *did* have the resources… or Aunt Shannon did. The magical nets she'd strung up around her back garden to ward off trespassers might have no effect on a magical beast compared to a bird or squirrel, but I'd sooner have eaten my sceptre than ask to borrow one.

"Yes, but we aren't obligated to share them with you." I abandoned all attempt at polite reasoning. "Especially if you want to risk your lives unnecessarily."

"I see Robin Wildwood has outvoted us." Acacia gave a laugh. "Perhaps she's afraid."

"I intended to go into the forest myself before you invited yourselves into my headquarters." I glared at her. "I did not agree to endanger anyone else."

"We're free to judge the risk for ourselves, are we not?" Isadora climbed decisively to her feet. "I assume the contents of your storeroom are open for anyone to use."

"Wait—" She wasn't wrong, but it was common courtesy to *ask* before borrowing another coven's props.

Without Jemima or my own coven members to back me up, though, I was outnumbered.

At Isadora's command, her fellow coven members rose to their feet and followed her from the room. Meanwhile, Acacia picked up the Seeing Stone and returned it to her bag. I might have objected, but I hadn't any desire to consult the stone with witnesses around. I'd have to wait until later—assuming Isadora didn't get clawed to death by the monster. *What is she thinking?*

When Acacia's people left, too, I gave up and returned to my office. Hearing the murmur of Mum and Jemima's voices, I strained to listen, but the general clamour of the other witches in the lobby prevented me from hearing a word.

Grandma's ghost appeared in front of me. "Busy here, isn't it?"

"Whoa." I took a startled step back. *I thought she was sulking.* "The other Head Witches have decided they're going into the forest to bait the monster into walking into a trap."

"Let them," she said. "At least if they're taking the risk, they can be blamed and not us."

"You know perfectly well that won't be the case," I said in a low voice. "We still own the forest, and Mavis nearly died yesterday. We can't let anyone else join her."

"The beast has been eluding the police all night, or so I heard," Grandma commented. "I doubt it'll show its face to the others."

"And if it does?" Perhaps two Head Witches put together would be able to fight off the beast, but if they did so and I wasn't present, then they'd take credit. My coven would be disgraced, my leadership cast in doubt—even more than it already was.

Grandma vanished when my office door opened and Jemima emerged with Mum behind her.

"They're going into the forest," I said quickly. "I couldn't stop them—"

"Couldn't?" Mum echoed.

Shame washed over me when Jemima gave me a disappointed look. Mum had already told her all about my lack of experience, of course, but she didn't have to undermine me in front of my one remaining ally among the Head Witches.

"I can't blast them with my sceptre every time they do something I don't like," I told my mother. "That's not the kind of Head Witch I want to be. I'll try to keep them away from danger, but I'd greatly appreciate it if I didn't have to do so alone."

The other Head Witches came sailing past, and my heart sank when I saw that two of Isadora's coven members carried one of Aunt Shannon's nets. *She gave them the bait. She wanted them to enter the forest.* Now I'd be on the hook if they failed… or worse.

Mum and Jemima watched with expressions of slight bemusement as the others left the building, as if they hadn't believed how committed Isadora and Acacia were to their plans.

"I think the police will set them straight," Mum said. "There's no need for us to join you."

Seriously? "Then I hope for all our sakes that the creature doesn't show up while they're rampaging around the woods. Also, Acacia stole the Seeing Stone from Mavis's room while she was unconscious. Thought you should know."

"What?" Helena wailed from inside the office.

I hadn't known Mavis's familiar was listening in, but a moment later, Tansy ran over to the door. "You aren't going into the forest, are you?"

"Someone has to stop them." I let Tansy climb onto my shoulder and then hurried to catch up with the others. I knew this wasn't a great idea, but there was no way I'd let the other Head Witches walk into the forest without me being present. The police wouldn't be pleased, and for all I knew, they'd be able to put a stop to Isadora's plan without my intervention, but it was better to be certain.

Either way, there was bound to be a kerfuffle, but anything was better than the creature showing up—

I came to an abrupt halt when we came within sight of the forest. Instead of the police, Tiffany Henbane, of all people, blocked the other Head Witches' advance.

I stand corrected.

"There's no need to go any farther," she announced. "We've caught the perpetrator."

I goggled at her. "What do you mean, *we?*"

"I mean myself and the police." She wore an expression of bitter satisfaction. "I found a shifter roaming around the clearing where Rachel was attacked, so I informed the police immediately."

What? "The attack happened days ago. Did you ambush a bystander to accuse them of murdering your coven member?"

The presence of the other Head Witches might have made me reluctant to confront her publicly, but I couldn't let this stand. Had she really convinced the police to arrest an innocent person?

Tiffany's gaze landed on the net in Isadora's hands. "What's all that for? Did you hope to catch the creature in a trap? I suppose it's worth a try, though it's a shame that *our* town's Head Witch has to be undermined."

Anger flooded me. "I think it's a shame that nobody can respect the police's orders to stay away from the sites of the attacks. You aren't supposed to be in the forest at all, Tiffany."

"Neither is that shifter." She stepped aside. "Feel free to judge for yourselves."

"Wait." I advanced, but the other witches were already on the forest path, exchanging tense whispers as they walked.

I hurried to overtake them and entered the clearing. There, a young blond shifter stood with his back against a tree, trapped between two other figures. One held a camera and the other a microphone, and my heart sank into my shoes as I recognised Clarice and Speck's bright-red cloaks.

12

Clarice and Speck turned towards me, wearing identical grins.

"Head Witch!" Clarice exclaimed. "You got here just in time. Would you like to give us a statement?"

White-hot anger surged through me, and my sceptre lit up a bright enough shade of purple that the reporters jumped behind a nearby tree to avoid being blinded.

"What exactly is this?" I demanded. "Who let you into the forest? I seem to remember banning you from Wildwood Heath myself, so you're breaking the law by being here."

"The forest isn't part of the town," Speck said from behind the tree, his voice trembling.

"It's the property of my coven," I corrected. "You're lucky the police haven't already arrested you."

"We were invited!" Clarice squeaked. "By—"

"Tiffany." Deep down, I hadn't believed my aunt when she'd claimed Tiffany was behind today's interview, but now she'd done far worse. "Whereabouts are the police, exactly?"

"I don't know!" Speck said. "We haven't seen them."

At least they hadn't arrested the shifter, but Tiffany must have intentionally distracted the police in order to smuggle the two journalists into town. I didn't know if she'd planned for the other Head Witches to witness the fallout, but she was all too happy to reap the benefits of duping everyone.

"There's absolutely no reason for you to show up when there's no news to report on," I told the journalists. "Get out."

"There is news." Clarice inched out from behind the tree. "We may have found the person to blame for the recent attacks."

"There's no proof whatsoever. All you're doing is hassling a member of the public."

"He was found at the scene of the crime," said Speck.

"Allegedly—and days after the attack actually took place." What would it take to get rid of these people? Pity there wasn't enough wildlife in the area for me to summon a swarm of birds to drive them off this time. "The police have been risking their lives looking for the creature responsible, and now they have to waste their time dealing with the two of you."

"So you admit there's a dangerous predator on the loose?" Clarice shuffled into view, her microphone in hand.

"No more dangerous than a wild boar or... or a wolf." The problem was, England didn't really *have* predators that were a danger to humans, except for magical ones. But none of those predators lived in the Wildwood.

"A dragon?" Clarice suggested, pushing her microphone in my direction. "Would you like to comment on the allegations that a group of dragons was recently brought into the Wildwood?"

"Untrue." I glared right into her camera lens. "There are no dragons here. They don't even like forests—they prefer open spaces. Will you get that microphone out of my face, please?"

Luckily for her, the police showed up before I blasted the microphone out of her hands altogether. The shifter, who'd retreated to the edge of the clearing, looked relieved instead of frightened. No doubt he was glad someone had come to rescue him from the reporters, even if he ended up being arrested in the process.

Not a chance. Spotting my brother, I called to him. "Ramsey, can your team please escort these reporters out of our forest?"

"How?" He looked between Clarice and Speck, a muscle twitching in his jaw. "How did they get here?"

"Tiffany," I said simply. "She distracted your team and ambushed a local shifter in an attempt to pin the blame on him."

I expected Tiffany to raise an objection, but when I looked behind me, I saw no sign of her. Knowing Tiffany, she'd crept out of the forest as soon as the police had come within sight... but the other Head Witches had vanished too. *Oh no.*

Ramsey exhaled. "I'll handle the reporters. You—go home."

"I can't. The other Head Witches took it upon themselves to come looking for the monster, and Tiffany let them into the forest."

"Where are you going?" One of the other officers approached the blond shifter, who'd turned away as if to leave the clearing. "We need to ask you some questions. What were you telling those reporters?"

"He's innocent," I told them. "The reporters were hassling him because Tiffany told them he was the culprit, based on no evidence."

"She set me up," the shifter added. "I was walking in the woods, and she ambushed me, claiming I was near a crime scene."

"Where is she?" Ramsey asked. "Tiffany?"

"She ran off, I assume." I backed up a step. "Look—I need to find the other Head Witches. They seem to think they can lure the monster into a trap, and I'd prefer to get them out of here before someone gets clawed to death."

I scanned the trees and caught sight of the gold sheen of Isadora's cloak. She and the other Head Witches had halted on a nearby path, crouching over what I assumed was their trap.

"You can't put that here." I strode over to them. "It's too close to human habitation. Besides, the police have ordered everyone to leave the forest."

If they'd decided to proceed with their plan to set up a trap for the monster, they presumably hadn't believed Tiffany's story about the shifter's guilt, but their timing couldn't have been worse if they'd tried.

"Not that witch you were talking to," said Acacia. "She's still in here."

"Tiffany Henbane," Isadora said. "I remember she was one of the favourites to become Head Witch."

"Who told you that?" I queried. "Nobody here thought

she had a chance, I can assure you. Now, please get out of this forest, or else I'll have to inform the police."

"How dare you—"

"She's right," Jemima said from behind me. "Leave the forest."

Relief washed over me that Jemima had come to back me up despite my mother's warnings, especially when Chloe came running to join her, breathless.

"My apologies, Head Witch," she gasped out. "I was delayed. Please let me escort your guests back to the inn."

Acacia's disdainful gaze travelled over our group. "There's no need for that. We can make our own way out."

"Yes, we can," Isadora agreed. "We'll come back later."

The two of them left the forest with their fellow coven members in tow, while Chloe bent double to catch her breath. She must have sprinted straight here from the coven's headquarters, and I wondered if Mum had downplayed just how much trouble I was in while she'd been in my office talking to Jemima.

Whatever they'd been talking about, it better have been urgent enough to justify throwing me to the wolves. Or witches, rather. I turned to Jemima to ask, only to see Mum herself approaching us at a brisk stride.

"Good," Mum said. "You convinced them to leave."

No thanks to you. "I may have damaged our professional relationship in the process, but they weren't going to back down unless I was direct with them."

"What's this about reporters in the forest?" Her nostrils flared. "Who called the press?"

"Ramsey's team is escorting them out of the forest," I said. "They were hassling a local shifter. Tiffany Henbane called them and then set up that shifter to take the fall.

She must have been thrilled when the Head Witches showed up too."

"You brought them into the forest yourself," Mum corrected. "I trusted you to take the situation into your own hands, but this is a disaster."

"You ordered me to follow procedures." I tried to hide the sting of her words, but hurt crept into my voice despite my best efforts. "There *is* no procedure for handling anything we've dealt with this week. Besides, I expected the police to back me up, but Tiffany drove them away from the path so she could sneak those reporters into town."

"Why a shifter?" Jemima asked. "Why frame one of them?"

"Tiffany is convinced a shifter was responsible for the attacks based on no evidence whatsoever," I told her. "As for the press, I expect they went along with her stories because it gives them something controversial to print. Not to mention an excuse to come back to Wildwood Heath."

Mum cleared her throat. "What's done is done. The reporters are being escorted out of the forest, and after that, the police will resume their search."

"Isadora said she'd be back later," I warned. "Acacia too. I don't know why they got it into their heads that they could lure the creature into a trap, but they seem to have taken my invitation to stay in town until Mavis recovers as permission to do as they like."

"If I know Acacia, she's calling the local branch of the paranormal hunters," said Jemima. "I'm surprised she hasn't already tried."

"She can't call the hunters to intervene in a community

she's not even a part of." I looked between her and Mum. "Can she? Don't answer that. We've wasted enough time on her and Isadora's whims already."

Frustration burned beneath my skin. This would normally be the point where random birds would start landing in the nearby trees, drawn by my anger, but nothing stirred except Tansy. "She can certainly try, but we'll send her packing," she ventured.

"She won't have the chance to," Mum said. "Because you're going to go and talk to her yourself and make it quite clear that our coven won't allow it. Right, Jemima?"

She's giving Jemima orders? I half expected the other Head Witch to argue. She outranked Mum, of course... but she'd also gone into our first meeting expecting Mum to be Head Witch and her equal. Not me.

"I will do my best to," Jemima answered. "I'll let you know how it goes."

While Jemima left, Tansy wrapped her tail around the back of my neck in her customary comforting gesture. "Those reporters had better not come back."

"I'd be more worried about them calling reinforcements." I directed this at Mum. "The other Head Witches were my priority at the time, but we have to make sure they know they aren't welcome here."

"You were correct to prioritise the Head Witches." Mum walked away, forcing me to hurry to keep pace with her. "That said, now they think our coven is unwelcoming at best, incompetent at worst."

"What else was I supposed to do?" I lowered my voice so that nobody would overhear us. "They decided to put together a trap, and Aunt Shannon was all too happy to help. I hardly expected the reporters to come here like a swarm of wasps and drive the police away from doing their jobs."

"Speaking of whom, every tabloid will have a field day with this," she said. "Ramsey and the police are going to have to clear up this mess themselves, and that unfortunate shifter will get the backlash that doesn't land on our family."

"You don't need to tell me that." I could picture the headlines all too clearly. "Tiffany set that shifter up, not me, and she's the one who called the reporters and drove the police away. I didn't do anything but try to stop them."

"Precisely. You didn't do enough."

Okay, that was enough. I'd been willing to take responsibility for my own choices, but she was acting as if I'd encouraged the others to go into the forest rather than the opposite. "Neither did you. Jemima stepped in before you lifted a finger to help your own daughter."

"You're *Head Witch*." The words rang out. "Did your grandmother ever ask her mother to take over duties from her?"

"I wouldn't know, would I? She doesn't tell me anything." A faint glow came to the sceptre in response to my agitation. "Head Witch or not, there's a limit to the ways in which I can use my authority against others. Acacia even stole the Seeing Stone from Mavis while she was in the hospital, so she doesn't respect the other Head Witches any more than she respects me."

"She did *what*?" Mum's mouth turned down at the corners. "Acacia was due to take the Stone next, was she? If so, given Mavis's current state, she acted within the rules."

"Funny how the rules sidestep all those pesky etiquette

lessons you drilled into me. Or even basic human decency."

"That, Robin, isn't a requirement of the job. You'd do well to remember that."

And with that, she overtook me, walking ahead and out of the forest. My eyes stung, angry tears threatening to spill. Tansy's tail snaked over my neck, and my sob turned into a laugh as she tickled my ear. "Stop it."

"Just trying to cheer you up."

"It's working." I wiped my eyes on the back of my hand. "Tiffany has gone too far this time though. Something has to be done."

"Exactly," Tansy agreed. "You don't want to find *her* next, do you?"

"Turning her into a frog will make me feel better."

Unfortunately, Tiffany was long gone, suffering no consequences for wasting the police's time. Instead, my mother blamed *me* for this mess.

"I vote we talk to Rowan instead," said Tansy.

The idea wasn't unappealing, if just because I desperately needed to find someone who *didn't* blame me for the current mess engulfing all of us. If nothing else, she might be able to help me come up with a suitable revenge plan for those reporters *and* Tiffany.

Rowan took one look at my face when she answered the door and said, "Want to play *Mario Kart?*"

"Yes, please."

When I'd followed her upstairs and closed her flat

door behind me, she added, "I'm guessing things with the other Head Witches didn't go as planned?"

"That's one way of putting it," I said. "If I even *had* a plan, it's officially jumped off a cliff without a broomstick."

"Ouch. What did they do?"

"Among other things, our favourite reporters are back in town, Tiffany has been accusing innocent bystanders of committing crimes, and I insulted all of our guests except two, one of whom is still in the hospital."

"Mavis hasn't woken up yet?"

"Not that I've heard." I walked over to the sofa and flopped into a pile of cushions in front of the TV. "Isadora and Acacia decided to search the forest themselves, and I had to resort to threatening them with arrest to get them to leave."

"And the reporters?"

"The police are escorting them out of town, but the damage is already done," I mumbled into the cushions. "Tiffany Henbane called them here and said we'd caught the culprit."

"No way." She joined me at the sofa and gave me a gentle shove to make room to sit down. "Who'd she blame?"

"A shifter she found in the forest." I shuffled into a sitting position, leaning back against the cushions. "She set the reporters on him. I hope the police let *him* go without punishment, but Tiffany ran off. This on top of the article the *Blue Moon* printed this morning."

"I saw." She grimaced. "I assumed that was my mother's work too."

"She denied it, blaming Tiffany." I swore under my

breath. "I bet she knew Tiffany was in the forest. I wondered why she loaned the other Head Witches one of her nets to catch the creature, aside from wanting to wind me up."

Her eyes widened. "They're still in the forest?"

"No. I drove them out, and Mum is mad at me for ruining the peace."

"At least the reporters have gone too." Rowan leaned forwards and turned on the TV, loading up her games console. "I guess I know why they didn't call me. They had more than enough material already."

"They still tried to push me into giving a statement," I said. "I guess they were irked that I blocked their numbers. They'll be back. Though I almost want them to stay in the forest and get eaten by that monster."

"I'm surprised the creature managed to stay hidden with that many people around."

"Someone is using magic to hide it, I think. Or using transportation spells to move it around, but I can't imagine any massive predator being fine with being transported magically all over the countryside against its will."

"Unless it jumped through a magical portal or something?" Rowan's expression turned thoughtful. "You know, if a spell is keeping it hidden, the person responsible must be pretty close by. Spells like that have a time limit."

"Who though?" I asked. "That's where I'm stuck. I don't think it's any of the other Head Witches."

"Can't you use that… what's it called, a Seeing Stone?"

"Acacia has it." I heaved a sigh. "She took it from Mavis's hotel room while she was unconscious in hospital, and now she'll have it for weeks. Besides, there's no chance she'll let me get my hands on it after I insulted her so thoroughly."

"You still need it?" Rowan picked up the games controller and tapped a few buttons, loading up the menu for *Mario Kart*. "Can't you borrow it while she isn't looking?"

"You don't think she'd notice if it disappeared from her room?" I raised a brow. "Besides, it didn't work for her."

"Or so *she* claimed." Rowan pushed the second controller into my hand. "I don't trust a single one of them."

"Neither do I, but I don't know that she'd have kept quiet if the Stone showed her the culprit. She'd want everyone to know." I scrolled through the character list and picked Yoshi, my favourite. "Also, she told everyone she doesn't actually believe the Seeing Stone showed the future."

"Maybe it only works for people who are open-minded." Rowan selected Bowser as her character. "Seriously, I think it's worth a shot."

"I can help you steal it," Tansy offered.

"Tansy, it's more than twice your size, and I bet it's immune to most spells, like conjuring or transportation. If it wasn't, the Stones would go missing more often."

"I'm stronger than I look." Tansy flexed her arms. "Go on, give me a shot."

The notion was tempting, I wouldn't lie, but was it worth risking being caught? Acacia had brought half her coven with her, and she probably slept with the Stone under her pillow.

"You can sneak in and out of Acacia's room, right?" I put down the controller to give my familiar my full attention. "I'd at least like to know if she decided to call the hunters, like Jemima thought she would."

"The hunters?" Rowan dropped her own controller. "Not the paranormal hunters?"

"They're Acacia's answer to everything," I explained. "She wants them to move into the area, since we don't have a local base, and this monster situation has only made her more convinced she's in the right."

"That might be the point." She reached down to retrieve her controller. "Are you sure she's not involved?"

"At this point, who knows." I shrugged and returned to the game. "Go on, Tansy. Might as well do something useful, other than dreading what stories the press will print about me tomorrow."

13

Tansy scurried off to the inn alone, while I waited in Rowan's flat and hoped that Acacia was too annoyed over being driven out of the forest to notice her furry trespasser. I also tried not to think about how I'd gone from being scared to let the Head Witches see the slightest flaw in my leadership to conspiring to steal their most valuable possession. Even if it was only on a temporary basis.

I was betting on the slim chance that Acacia had simply left the Stone in her hotel room and then gone elsewhere, no doubt to plot new ways to weasel in on the investigation. I certainly hadn't foreseen her and Isadora joining forces, but if one of them actually did call the hunters, we had a new set of problems on our hands. I hoped that was a needless worry, because if she made the call, she'd have to admit her own failures to find the creature herself.

Really, with the forest full of police officers, reporters

running around, and Tiffany Henbane on the loose, I almost didn't blame the monster for staying hidden.

I won three games of *Mario Kart* in a row before Tansy scurried back through the open window.

"I don't see the Seeing Stone in her room," she said. "Either she gave it to someone else, or she hid it in her luggage."

"Figures." I put the controller down. "You know, I could try conjuring up the Seeing Stone with the sceptre to see what happens, but it's bound to have protections on it."

"Might be worth the risk," Rowan commented. "Not that you want to set off any magical alarms."

"No, I really don't." I pulled a face. "Tansy, the others weren't talking about contacting the hunters or sneaking into the forest again, were they?"

"No," Tansy said. "I think they put that plan aside in the meantime, but Acacia is in Isadora's hotel room with half the council, talking strategies."

Thought so. "But they aren't using the Seeing Stone."

If the Stone wasn't in the room with them, might I be able to get away with conjuring it from Acacia's luggage? It was worth a shot.

As I reached for the sceptre, a flash of green caught my eye from near the open window. The instant I picked up the sceptre, Helena the toad came soaring through the window and landed on my outstretched hand.

Rowan stared at me. "Why is there a toad in my flat?"

"She's Mavis's familiar," I explained. "She's supposed to be in my office. Helena, what are you doing here?"

"It won't do any good for you to conjure the Seeing

Stone," Helena croaked. "Everyone will know the instant you do."

"Have you been following me all this time?" I leaned the sceptre against the sofa and lifted the quivering toad into the air. "Why?"

"I want to see if Mavis is any better," she croaked. "And that cat in your office keeps looking at me as if she wants to eat me."

Probably because she does. At least I'd been fore-warned about the Seeing Stone, but as tempting as it might have been to spend the rest of the day playing video games with Rowan, the other Head Witches hadn't ceased their scheming. I needed a new strategy.

"I'll take you to the hospital then," I said to Helena. "We'll see if Mavis is awake, but I wouldn't get your hopes up."

"Good call," Rowan said. "I'm here if you need anything else, all right?"

"Thanks." I picked up the sceptre and made for the door, Tansy on my heels.

Outside the café, I looked up and down the street and spied my mother approaching from the direction of the police station. Oh boy. She'd already spotted me, so I resigned myself to another awkward encounter.

Mum strode towards me. "Robin, what are you doing here?"

"I was gaming with Rowan until Helena climbed through the window." I held up the toad. "She wants to know if Mavis is awake yet."

"She is."

"Wait... she is?" Relief swept over me, punctured

immediately by wariness when Mum's grim expression didn't change. "Does she remember the attack?"

"No," Mum said briskly. "According to the members of her coven who spoke to her, Mavis claims the monster attacked her from behind. She used her sceptre to cast a defensive spell, which hit the nearby trees, but Mavis fell unconscious immediately afterwards."

"That makes no sense." How could any creature have inflicted such wounds and then vanished into thin air? "Was there anyone else in the area? Human or otherwise?"

"You'll have to ask her yourself," Mum said. "Later, that is. The hospital isn't allowing visitors from outside of her coven."

Helena squirmed in my hands. "I have to see her"

"Wait a moment." I held onto the wriggling toad with difficulty. "Mum, I assume the hospital will let her familiar in?"

"I didn't ask."

So our earlier argument was still bothering her then. "I'll take that as a yes—whoa."

I staggered back when Helena gave a flying leap out of my hands and began hopping frantically in the direction of the hospital.

"That toad is a lot more aerodynamic than she looks," Tansy remarked.

"I hope nobody treads on her," I said. "Anyway, she's not going to be the only person clamouring to get into Mavis's room when the others find out."

"I'd advise you to avoid the inn." Mum turned away. "Ramsey is back at the police station if you want to apologise to him."

"Apologise for what?" I was probably wasting my time

trying to figure that one out, so I walked the short distance to the police station.

With Tansy at my back, I entered the lobby via the automatic doors and made straight for my brother's office. I hadn't intended to lose Mavis's familiar again, but at least I had one fewer worry on my hands if she remained at the hospital instead of in my office.

Ramsey looked askance at me across his desk. "What is it, Robin? If you've finally come to get rid of those reporters, they've already gone."

"What?" I blinked. "No, I haven't. It might have escaped your attention, but I was trying to handle three emergencies at once back there. Getting the Head Witches out of the forest was my priority, so I had to leave the reporters for your team to handle. Also, have you sent anyone after Tiffany yet?"

"No, I haven't. You aren't the only one dealing with multiple crises."

He wasn't wrong. "It would help if our mother didn't criticise every decision I made. Did she tell you Mavis woke up?"

"Yes, and that she isn't allowed visitors."

"I'm more concerned with the fact that she didn't see the monster that attacked her."

"Yes." His gaze dropped to a stack of papers on his desk. "It's perplexing. I don't know what you expected me to say, Robin, but I have no other information."

What had I expected? My argument with Mum had put me on the defensive, which didn't help, but I was honestly more annoyed with myself than I was with anyone else. My attempts to avoid the press had led to them camping on my doorstep, while my quest to make the other Head Witches see me as their equal had come back to bite me too. And if I'd just accepted Mavis's help in the first place, we might have found the creature responsible for the attacks without anyone else getting hurt.

"Sorry, Ramsey." I sighed. "I know you're snowed under, but Tiffany had no good reason to be in the forest. She set up that shifter—what happened to him, anyway?"

"He's giving a statement," Ramsey said. "If he wants us to call in Tiffany for setting the press on him, we'll send someone to search for her, but our resources are stretched thin."

"I know." Why did I get the feeling that time was running out? Oh, right, because I'd said the meeting would be postponed until Mavis woke up, working under the assumption that she'd be able to point the finger at her attacker when she did so. I hadn't expected her not to remember, nor had I banked on Acacia claiming the Seeing Stone in the interim.

In my pocket, my phone began to buzz.

"I'll see you later." I retreated from Ramsey's office. "I swear, if this is the press, I'll shove that microphone—"

Tansy stuck her head out of my pocket. "It's Harvey."

"Oh." I fished out my phone one-handed and answered the call as I crossed the lobby. "Hey, Harvey."

"Hey, Robin," Harvey said. "Are you okay?"

"Yeah… sorry, it's been kind of a manic day." The automatic doors slid open, and Tansy ran outside ahead of me.

"I heard," he said. "About the press, I mean. They tried to sneak back into town?"

"Because someone invited them," I said. "To be precise, Tiffany Henbane did. She also ambushed a random shifter to frame for the attacks and set the press on them. Oh, and the other Head Witches saw the whole thing, because they wanted to hunt down the monster themselves and wouldn't take no for an answer."

"Wait, they did?" he asked. "Are they in the forest? With the reporters?"

"No, they're back at the inn. As for the reporters, they're probably camping on the hillside."

"That doesn't sound particularly safe."

"I'm not all that fussed if they get eaten." Not that that would do much to help my cause, but there was little I could do to get rid of them entirely, short of giving them the interview they so desperately wanted. "The police sent them packing, but they're supposed to be looking for our elusive monster, not fending off the press."

After our encounter in the forest, Clarice and Speck wouldn't even need to make up outrageous lies to paint me as incompetent. I might at least have tried harder to defend the dragons against their accusations, but what else could I have told them? The truth was out of the question. Some of it was, anyway.

"True," said Harvey. "What do you want to do, meet up? I can be at Were's My Coffee? in five."

"Sure." I ended the call and scrolled down my phone's screen, catching sight of Clarice's number in my recent call list. If she and Speck had expected me to do anything but send them packing, they'd been seriously lying to themselves. Then again, wasn't lying what they did best?

Well... they didn't exactly lie when they mentioned the drag-ons. Whoever had told tales on us had given them enough of the truth for them to twist to their own agenda.

I halted outside the café, recalling being ambushed by

reporters in this very spot. They were utterly relentless, but I felt worse for the shifter they'd interviewed. He'd been set up, but anyone who watched the interview wouldn't see it that way, and he didn't have the protection of a coven the way I did.

Harvey showed up within minutes, greeting me with a hug and a brief kiss. "You look lost in thought. What's up?"

"I must be losing my mind," I admitted. "But can I borrow your phone and call the press myself? They won't know your number, so you shouldn't get bombarded with calls afterwards. If you do, you can just block them like I did."

"You want to call them?" His brow furrowed. "Sure, you can borrow my phone, if you're sure."

"I'm not sure, but let's get this done before I change my mind."

Maybe I was losing my mind, but if setting up an interview with Clarice and Speck myself would take the heat off the shifter Tiffany had framed, it might be worth the trade-off. If nothing else, I might be able to set the record straight before anyone else went to jail for the killer's crimes. Let's face it, I'd already given the reporters the worst possible impression of our family. I could hardly sink any lower.

Not that I was keen to tempt fate.

Harvey and I picked out a table in the far corner, and he handed me his phone. My family wouldn't be thrilled at me for talking to the press without their input, but hadn't I already done exactly that? More to the point, if I gave the full story of the incident with the dragons, I might even be able to improve our family's image a little.

Harvey gave my shoulder a reassuring squeeze as I typed in Clarice's number and hit the call button.

Clarice's cheery voice answered at once. "Hello?"

"Clarice," I said. "This is the Head Witch, Robin Wildwood. I've changed my mind about that interview."

Her squeal of excitement was loud enough that everyone in the vicinity looked up from their coffees in alarm.

"Tone it down," I hissed. "I'll speak to you *only* if I can do the interview on my terms."

"Of course!" Speck's muffled voice came from behind Clarice's excited breathing. "Which number are you calling from?"

"I borrowed a friend's phone, someone who has no idea who you are." I had no qualms about telling a few white lies to stop them from hassling Harvey in future. "Are you still in the woods?"

"Don't worry, we're far away from that mysterious monster of yours. That's what you want to discuss, isn't it?"

Nice try. "We'll save it for the interview, shall we? I'll let you know my conditions before we start. Firstly, this interview is the only one I'll give you. If you intend to print an article about me, then you're free to quote this interview, but nothing else. Including our encounter earlier. No spinning my words to make it sound like I was in the wrong and not you."

"Well, of course." Some of the excitement had faded from Clarice's voice. "Is that all?"

"No," I said. "You aren't to mention that shifter you interviewed earlier at all. He was an innocent bystander, nothing more. Also, if I talk to you, then I speak on behalf of the rest of my family—all of them. There'll be no need to interview anyone else in the Wildwood Coven. Break your word, and I'll have full authority to ban you from the Wildwood indefinitely."

"That won't be necessary." She sounded peevish. "All we wanted was your story."

"And you'll get it," I said. "If you agree to the terms, we'll start now. I'll give you an hour, no more."

"Fine," said Clarice, all business. "Let's begin."

The questions were standard to start off with, mostly concerning how I'd felt about my first official meeting with the Head Witches. I didn't have to lie when I said I'd been nervous but keen to get to work. *Or to get it over with. Whichever works.*

As I'd expected, Clarice and Speck were very interested in what exactly I'd been doing the previous week.

"My mother, brother, and I went to visit one of the other Head Witches so I could meet her prior to the meeting." Not a lie. "On the way, we found a wild dragon hatchling that had been separated from its parents. Our family has an affinity with animals, so we decided to extend our journey and reunite it with its parents. We did so, relocating their whole family to a remote colony in the south of England."

"Interesting," Clarice said. "So you didn't bring it near the Wildwood?"

"No," I said firmly. "Dragons prefer open spaces to enclosed forests, and we had no intention of releasing the animals close to human habitation. Our detour extended our trip by a couple of days, but we flew home immediately afterwards."

"Then you had your meeting with the Head Witches,

right?" Speck's muffled voice asked from the background. "Can you tell us more?"

"I can't share the classified details of our meeting." That and I doubted they'd be interested. No, the real story lay in what had happened next, and I had no intention of dancing around the subject. "Afterwards, my mother and I took the other Head Witches for a prearranged tour of the town. When we entered the Wildwood, we found that a member of another local coven had been attacked and killed by what appeared to be a dangerous magical predator. Naturally, we called the police right away."

"And?" Clarice sounded a little breathless. "You must tell us more. The monster attacked a Head Witch next, didn't it?"

"The police searched the forest the best they could, but it was near dark before long," I went on. "They resumed the search the following day while I held another meeting with the other Head Witches. Afterwards, I went to help with the search. Since the forest is too large to cover on foot, I decided to use my broomstick to search from the sky. I saw a disturbance below and immediately descended, but I arrived too late to see the creature. It had attacked Head Witch Mavis Willow and vanished."

"The other Head Witch survived?" Speck asked, his voice hushed.

"Yes, she did," I replied. "She's recovering in hospital. Due to the attack, I decided to postpone our last meeting while I helped the police search the forest. Unfortunately, when I reached the Wildwood, I found the police had been driven away from their search. Among other disturbances, a pair of reporters was roaming around the woods."

Clarice coughed. "Really, we were invited. We didn't break any laws."

Tiffany did. A rush of impatience seized me. Perhaps I should have gone to confront Tiffany rather than agreeing to this interview, but knowing her, she was lying low until she was certain the police had forgotten her transgression.

"Can this part be off the record?" I asked. "I have a question I want to ask you."

"What?" I could imagine Clarice's frown on the other end of the phone. "Isn't this supposed to be an interview with the Head Witch?"

"I think it's only fair that you tell me who called you," I said. "I'm not the one with the recording equipment, so I can agree not to share anything you tell me. Who invited you into the forest?"

Speck answered. "Tiffany called us with the news that she'd found a suspect at the scene of the crime and that a shifter was behind the attacks, not a magical beast at all. The shifter we found in the forest denied her accusations. That's all there is to it."

"It'd better be. Back to the interview."

"Yes." Clarice's voice lacked its usual enthusiasm. "In the time since you've been Head Witch, we've heard all manner of rumours about your lack of experience for the role. Would you like to address those comments?"

"Yes." I caught Harvey's eye, and he gave me a reassuring nod. "You forget that I wasn't voted into the position, and they don't test for fitness for the role when one picks up the sceptre. However, one might say the same of any Head Witch who's ever held the title."

"Including your grandmother?"

"Yes, her too." No point in denial at this stage. "Every other Head Witch was chosen in the same manner, including the ones who trespassed into the forest against my orders and the one who was near-fatally wounded earlier this week." I drew in a breath. "There's no other requirement. It might not make a good story, but it's true. Anyone else might have stood in my place, but as it stands, I intend to do my duty as Head Witch until the title is no longer mine. Anything else?"

"That... will do." Clarice sounded faint for some reason. "The interview is over."

14

When the call ended, Harvey gave me a concerned look. "Er… are you okay?"

"Yeah." When I stood up, adrenaline thrummed through my veins, and I sank back into my seat. "That was a lot. Maybe I shouldn't have been that harsh, but I don't remember Grandma ever pulling her punches in interviews either."

Perhaps she was the one I should have been taking cues from instead of my mother. Though considering she was currently hiding from the other Head Witches, she might not have been the best example to follow.

Harvey checked the time. "I have to give a lesson at the academy in ten minutes, so I need to run. Will you be okay?"

"Yeah, I think so." I walked with him to the café door. "I'll have to be patient and wait for the hospital to allow visitors in before I can see Mavis, but I should let my assistant know first. I kind of left her behind earlier."

After we parted ways, I went back to the witches'

headquarters, where Grandma greeted me by opening the office door with a gust of wind generated by flapping her arms wildly.

"I've been practising that for weeks," she said proudly.

"Good for you," I said. "Mavis is awake, but she doesn't remember her attacker, and the hospital isn't letting visitors in yet. Where's Chloe?"

"I haven't the faintest idea."

"What?" I thought back to when I'd last seen her. "She ought to have come back here after escorting the other Head Witches back to the inn."

In answer, a cup jumped off the desk and threw itself at me. Grandma cackled, while I caught the cup in my hand and placed it back on my desk.

"This is serious, Grandma," I said. "I have less than a day to find out who attacked Mavis and killed Rachel before the other Head Witches either leave town or try setting up another trap and catch it themselves."

"Trap." She scoffed. "If it's evaded all your efforts so far, I doubt a trap would hold it."

"I don't see you falling over yourself to help." I scanned the office and spotted the guide to magical creatures I'd left on my desk. Since it hadn't been much help, I returned it to the shelf I'd originally found it on. "I cannot figure out how a wild animal sneaked up on a Head Witch without being detected."

"Maybe she wasn't paying attention."

"Really helpful." I studied the titles on the bookshelf as if the answer would leap out at me if I stared hard enough.

"Don't think so hard. Your brain will overheat."

"That's not a thing, Grandma." I groaned when one of

the books jumped off the shelf. "And please stop playing at being a poltergeist."

"I'm far too important to be a mere poltergeist."

"Uh-huh." Wait a moment. "What… what if that's why we can't find the monster? It's like a ghost—invisible?"

"You think a ghost attacked two Head Witches?" Grandma made a sceptical noise.

"One," I corrected. "The first victim wasn't a Head Witch, and the second was taken by surprise. Poltergeists don't have claws, true, but they aren't the only beasts in the afterworld, are they?"

"I wouldn't know."

"Grandma, you've *been* to the afterworld." I returned my attention to the bookshelves, scanning for any available titles on ghosts and other spirits. "Do you have any resources here on summoning ghosts and the like?"

"Obviously. Any witch can summon a ghost."

I gave the shelves another scan and picked out a basic guide to ghosts and other spirits, skimming through the pages. Nothing in the book appeared to reference invisible beasts, but I halted on the glossary, a chill racing down my spine. "And if it's not a regular ghost? Might they have used necromancy instead?"

Grandma gave a theatrical shudder. "No, I most certainly do *not* have a guide to necromancy in my office. It's forbidden."

"You don't say."

Even the average Head Witch had little knowledge of necromancy, mostly because it was illegal to even try it. Meddling with the dead was a dodgy area at the best of times, and while summoning ghosts wasn't expressly forbidden, they didn't teach that kind of magic at the academy. Even the note in the book's glossary said, "Necromancy is a branch of magic concerning the dead and is utterly forbidden by most magical communities." Nothing more.

"Don't you even think about poking your nose into illegal magic," Grandma reprimanded me. "Most witches who meddle in necromancy face a grim death."

"I know." I studied her transparent form. "There's a difference between ghosts visible in the waking world and ones who've moved on. You've seen it for yourself, right?"

"You mean the true afterworld." Grandma drifted over to me as I placed the book on the desk in case I needed it later. "Yes. *That* place is off limits to anyone but the dead, and there are beasts that even ghosts fear to cross. If someone has dared to cross that line, then it will spell disaster for all of us."

"All the more reason for me to stop them."

If none of the books in Grandma's office contained the right information, then I had no choice but to visit the one surviving witness who might know what we were dealing with.

Closing the door on Grandma's protests, I left the office behind. Even if Mavis didn't have much to add to what I'd already heard, it was worth finding out if she remembered anything she hadn't shared with her coven members.

Did the other Head Witches have any similar suspicions? Surely not. They'd tried to catch the creature in a net, and I doubted any kind of trap could hold a beast that didn't have a physical form. *Wait.*

Tansy scurried alongside me. "Necromancy? Are you sure?"

"You said the whole forest felt creepy, right?" I recalled. "Those pigeons called it 'wrong.' Necromancy goes against nature. It fits."

Tansy's ears pricked. "You're right. I've never been near a necromancer before, but animals always know."

"Even those ridiculous pigeons, I guess."

"Yes, and especially red squirrels."

"That goes without saying."

Once we reached the high street, I veered towards the hospital. The blond receptionist leapt to her feet in alarm when she saw the sceptre in my hand.

"Head Witch," she said. "Sorry, we can't let you in. Mavis isn't allowed visitors—no exceptions."

Guessing I wasn't the first Head Witch to try sneaking in, I said, "I understand, but this is urgent. I think I've worked out what attacked Mavis, but I need to talk to her for a minute to confirm my theory before I tell the police. Is her familiar still in here? I can talk to her instead."

"I'm afraid she won't leave her witch's side."

"Let her in." Mavis's voice drifted from down the corridor, weaker than before but unmistakeable.

"Are you okay?" I took an uncertain step in that direction and was unsurprised when a nurse came hurrying to block my path.

Tansy had other ideas. She sprinted underneath the nurse's arm, ducking in and out of the staff members' attempts to catch her. I followed at a fast stride, reaching the private ward, where Mavis sat upright in bed. Helena perched on her bedside table, while Tansy hopped up to join her.

"Don't throw her out," Mavis told the nurses behind me. "I want to talk to Robin alone."

Wait. She does? Maybe she hadn't been willing to share her recollections with anyone else, but a pang of guilt hit me for not trusting her from the get-go.

The staff moved to obey. When the door closed, Mavis sat up straighter. "I hoped you'd show up sooner, but I suppose my well-meaning fellow coven members put you off."

My chest tightened at the sight of her thick bandages. "Sorry."

"Takes more than that to bring me down." She coughed. "I was a fool, going into the forest alone, but I thought it was a mere beast I was looking for."

"It wasn't a regular beast at all." I lowered my voice. "Right? Do you know what it was, exactly?"

The faintest creak from near the door made both of us turn in that direction.

"Someone's listening in," said Mavis. "Not that it matters if the other Head Witches find out. They've been waiting for me to drop dead, no doubt, but I'll be out of here by tomorrow."

"I delayed the meeting to pressure them into staying," I told her. "Mostly because I couldn't rule out any of the other witches as the culprits. Do you know if any of them might have been involved?"

"No." She shook her head. "No, even Isadora and Acacia haven't the faintest clue what we're dealing with."

"You mean—necromancy." I dropped my voice. "The truth is, I don't know anything either. We don't have any experts in the coven, not that I'm aware of."

"Most don't," she said. "If I were you, I'd call in a Reaper."

"A—" *Reaper?* "We don't have one. Not in this town, anyway."

Reapers were an oddity, even by the standards of the paranormal world. In theory, every region had at least one local Reaper, but I didn't personally know our nearest. They had almost nothing to do with the covens except when they came to collect our souls when one of us died, and since nobody had prevented Grandma from coming back as a ghost, they couldn't be that close to Wildwood Heath, surely.

Then again, it would be just like Grandma to have ignored the local Reaper's pleas for her to move on to the next world. It also wouldn't surprise me if she flat-out refused to let me invite one to town to deal with our current threat. Nothing would turf the former Head Witch out of her office, not even death itself.

"A Reaper is your best bet for dealing with the dead, but it's not the only option." Mavis coughed. "I'm afraid I won't be much help myself. I tired myself out listening in on the other Head Witches' conversations when they tried to get into my ward."

"No, you need to rest," I told her. "Also, I don't know if you heard, but Acacia has claimed your Seeing Stone and is ready to take it with her when she leaves town."

"She did what?" Outrage flickered across her expression. "So that's why she was so smug earlier."

"She tried to use the Stone to find the creature and didn't see anything useful," I said. "Allegedly, anyway. Which is annoying because I wanted to borrow it myself."

"I'd offer, but... well."

"It doesn't matter now," I said. "You just concentrate

on getting better, and I'll try to find out more about the creature in the woods."

And who'd summoned it. That was the pertinent question, because if necromancy was little known even among the Head Witches, identifying the monster in the forest would be tricky without the aid of an expert. Meaning a Reaper. Even the paranormal hunters would be worse than useless in this situation, given that none of them could even *see* ghosts. Let alone invisible monsters.

A nurse pushed open the door. "I have to give you your medicine, Head Witch."

"I'm just leaving," I told her. "Mavis, I'll see you later."

As Tansy hopped off the bedside table, Helena croaked, "I want to come with you."

"All right." I scooped her up in my free hand and walked out of the ward.

"Good luck," Mavis called after me.

I'll need it. With Helena in one hand and the sceptre in the other, I left the hospital behind. "I think we should let the police know what we're up against before we do anything else."

"Agreed." Tansy scampered ahead of me and nearly collided with a blond shifter. To be precise, the unlucky shifter that Tiffany had cornered in the forest.

"Head Witch." His eyes widened, both at the sceptre and at the toad sitting in my hand. "Ah, thanks for getting those reporters away from me earlier."

"No problem," I said. "The police didn't give you any trouble, did they?"

"No, they knew I was in the wrong place at the wrong time." He lowered his gaze. "I hope they did, anyway. I was taking a walk in the woods when that witch showed up and started yelling at me. I didn't know I was anywhere near the scene of the attack on that other witch."

"You probably weren't. Tiffany was looking for a target, and you were just unlucky enough to be in her way." I'd have to deal with *her* later. She wouldn't be allowed to get away with obstructing the police at every turn, not on my watch. When the shifter looked crestfallen, I added, "I did an interview with the press myself and cleared up the matter, and they won't use any of the video footage from the forest in their reports."

His expression brightened. "Thanks, Head Witch."

"Anytime." I walked past him, entering the police station.

Ramsey's office door stood ajar, and as I crossed the lobby, he stepped out and gave me a familiar long-suffering look. "You didn't ambush Ollie, did you?"

"You mean the shifter?" I asked. "Only to reassure him that the press aren't going to use any of the footage they recorded in the forest."

"And how would you know that?"

"I told them myself," I said. "I set the record straight, but that isn't the important part. I also spoke to Mavis—"

"You spoke to *who*?" He narrowed his eyes when he spotted Helena in my hand. "I thought you were going to stay at Rowan's today and keep out of trouble."

"I found out what's loose in the woods and why the police can't find it." I approached his office. "I'll tell you in here."

With visible reluctance, Ramsey joined me inside his office. "What is it? What's in the forest?"

"A ghost," said Tansy, while Helena trembled in my hand.

"Not a ghost exactly," I clarified. "I think someone in town has been dabbling in necromancy and summoned something they couldn't get rid of. Or maybe they didn't want to get rid of it. Not sure which."

The person who'd summoned the creature had risked their own safety as much as anyone else's, after all.

The colour drained from his face. "You can't be serious."

"It makes sense," I pressed. "If it's incorporeal, then it would explain how the creature has avoided detection."

"Incorporeal?" he echoed. "It attacked Mavis—and Rachel too. No ghost can leave marks on someone."

"Some poltergeists can, but I think it's more dangerous than that," I said. "Mavis suggested calling a Reaper, but the alternative is to find the summoner and convince them to tell us what they did."

"The summoner?" He blinked a couple of times. "If you're right… but who might it be? One of the other Head Witches?"

"Not according to Mavis." Who else did that leave though? "Have you sent anyone to question Tiffany yet?"

"No, we haven't." His expression sharpened. "You think she did it?"

Did I? I still didn't know if Tiffany would really have killed one of her own people, but it was exactly like her coven to do something reckless like dabbling in necromancy without considering the potential consequences. Whether or not she'd been involved in person, her commitment to accusing the shifters made more sense if she'd been trying to throw the police off the trail of the real culprit.

The trouble was, summoning ghosts didn't always

leave traces. Necromancy might, but if the creature had been summoned in the depths of the Wildwood, the odds of stumbling upon evidence were slim.

Ramsey lowered his gaze to the desk. "Regardless of who's responsible, half my team is still in the forest, and the rest are preparing to speak to Mavis now that she's awake. I can't spare anyone to go and find Tiffany."

"I'd find her myself, but—wait, have you seen my assistant?"

"Chloe?" he echoed. "She went back to the witches' headquarters with our mother."

Of course she had. "Right. I'll find her, but I think someone in the Henbane Coven is responsible for this, if not Tiffany herself. If she suspects I know, then we need to act quickly before she covers her tracks."

I was finally on the right track, I was sure, but I was running against the clock if I wanted answers before the other Head Witches left town. Or worse—before they found out too.

After leaving the police station, I broke into a jog. Tansy ran alongside me down the high street, while Helena sat on my hand and groaned at me for jostling her.

"You're making me nauseous," she objected.

"Please don't throw up on me," I said, breathless. "I don't have time to deal with a travelsick toad. Besides, don't you want me to find Mavis's attacker?"

That quietened her down, and we reached the witches' headquarters without any unfortunate mishaps. My office was as empty as I'd left it, so I carried Helena to my mother's office door instead of my own.

I took a page out of Mum's book and simply pushed

open the door without knocking. Three voices fell silent when I walked in—Chloe, Mum, and Jemima.

"Am I not invited to the meeting?" I looked between them. "Whatever you're talking about, I assume it's not for my ears, but I have some information I think you'll all want to hear."

15

Mum, Chloe, and Jemima all listened without comment as I told them everything I'd concluded so far. When I'd finished speaking, Chloe sprang to her feet and ran to search the bookshelves at the back of Mum's office. They were considerably tidier than Grandma's.

"I know there's a book on ghosts somewhere here." She ran her fingers across a row of titles. "Right, Mrs Wildwood?"

"This isn't a ghost at all," Mum said. "If it's true, then someone has taken a terrible gamble with the lives of the citizens of the town."

"Mavis thinks it's true," I said. "It explains why nobody has been able to track the creature down."

"You brought Mavis's familiar?" asked Jemima, seeing the toad climb onto my shoulder. Tansy sat on the other, her fluffy tail twitching.

"She wants to help bring in the culprit," I explained.

"Which is probably a better idea than hunting the beast itself without knowing what it is."

Chloe took a step back from the bookshelves. "I was sure there was a guide to summoning ghosts in here."

"I have a textbook on ghosts and spirits," I said. "Well, Grandma does, anyway."

"I imagine she borrowed it from me." Mum looked a little disgruntled. "Right, we'll relocate to your office. It's bigger."

It was also more crowded, but at least she'd called the office mine and not Grandma's. Baby steps. I led the way, and the other three followed me.

Inside the office, Grandma hovered above my desk, several books floating in the air around her. Including the one I needed. I grabbed the book out of the air, while Jemima looked at Grandma without any surprise in her expression. "Head Witch. It's good to see you again."

The books toppled to the floor while Grandma folded her arms across her chest. "What is everyone doing in here?"

I ignored her complaints and held up the book. "I think this has instructions on how to summon and banish ghosts, but I don't know if the same kind of spell was used to summon… whatever we're dealing with. The only reference to necromancy is in the glossary."

"It's not *summoning* the creature that concerns us," Mum said. "Rather, the opposite."

"To do that, we'd need to *find* it," Chloe said in a tremulous voice. "At the risk of any of us being attacked. It must still be in the forest, right?"

"I think so, but it can't be too far from its summoner." Goosebumps rose on my arms. "Though I have absolutely no idea if the person who summoned it has any control over the creature whatsoever. She's not known for thinking things through."

"Tiffany Henbane?" Mum asked. "You've been wrong about her before."

Did she mind Jemima knowing all this? She hadn't said, but our coven's rivalry with the Henbanes wasn't exactly a secret.

"I have," I acknowledged, "but if not her, it's someone in her coven. Rachel might have been set up to take the fall. It's not the first time Tiffany has thrown an apprentice into the line of fire."

Tansy sat upright on my shoulder. "Do you think Rachel is the one who summoned the creature?"

"She... she might have." I thought back to the state we'd found the clearing in. "She might not have known it'd attack her. I bet Tiffany didn't warn her."

"There's one way to find out," said Jemima. "If the creature *was* summoned in the clearing, it would have left a mark that can be detected using magic even if the summoner was careful to remove all other evidence."

"Really?" I knew how to cast a detection spell, but I hadn't thought to use one in the clearing. "I'll have another look around then. If Tiffany's there... I don't think Ramsey took me entirely seriously when I told him to send someone after her."

"I'll remind him myself." Mum pulled out her mobile phone. "Chloe, watch the Henbane Coven's headquarters for any movement."

"Good call." I made for the cupboard at the back of the office which contained Grandma's ingredient supplies. "I'll take some sage with me, just in case."

Sage repelled ghosts. It might not be strong enough to do the same to whatever beast we were looking for, but I didn't plan on meeting it face-to-face yet. Sage in hand, I left a reluctant Helena on my desk and beckoned Tansy to follow me out of the office.

Mum followed. "It's too risky to go in there alone."

"I thought you wanted me to do everything myself." I glanced through my office door, where Jemima stood watching my grandmother's ghost. "What were you two talking to Chloe about, anyway?"

"How to manage the fallout of this," Mum said. "The press, for one. We'll have to set up an interview—"

"I already did that," I said. "When I was at Rowan's. Harvey helped me by loaning me his phone so that I didn't have to unblock Clarice's number."

Mum blinked at me. "You did?"

"Yes, I did. I also ensured they wouldn't slander the shifter Tiffany tried to frame, and I made it quite clear that mine was the last interview they'd do with anyone in our family until the case is dealt with."

"Anyone?"

"Yes, including your sister—who's going to be in serious trouble if she turns out to have known about any of this."

"I doubt necromancy would have crossed her mind as a possibility." She scrolled through numbers on her phone and selected Ramsey's. "Go ahead if you must, but please be careful."

"I will." I let Tansy take the lead, heading for the path leading into the forest.

I half expected to run into Tiffany again, but the path

seemed to be deserted. Tansy ran ahead of me, ears pricked. "There's nobody out there."

"For now."

I followed the path and slowed when we reached the clearing where we'd found Rachel's body. For the police not to have found any evidence, she must have hidden it well, but none of the police officers carried a sceptre. Any spell I used would be boosted far beyond its normal levels. Recalling the movements for a revealing charm, I gave the sceptre a wave.

A bright light flared up around the sceptre's end. *Whoa.*

Like a picture coming into focus, marks appeared on the ground, spreading across the earth. Jagged lines, forming a star-like shape. A pentagram.

"Watch out!" Tansy squeaked in alarm.

A rumbling growl echoed around the clearing, seeming to come out of thin air. *Oh no.*

As I watched, a patch of darkness spread across the pentagram's surface like a shadow cast by something unseen. A semi-transparent creature took form within the black, a massive beast with slavering teeth and a shaggy coat, like a cross between a wolf and a bear. Definitely not a ghost nor anything else I'd seen in a textbook. The breath flew from my lungs, and terror gripped my limbs.

When its beastly eyes fixated on me, I waved the sceptre and cast the first spell that came into my head—a levitating charm.

The spell flew wide, missing the creature entirely as it launched towards me. Claws swiped inches away from my face. I threw myself flat to the ground and waved the sceptre, casting an immobilising spell. The beast stopped mid-motion, giving me the chance to scramble to my feet, but within two seconds, the creature growled, shaking off the spell's effects.

That shouldn't be possible. How could that creature have just shrugged off a spell that could keep even a Head Witch frozen for hours at a time? Disbelief flitted through my mind in the moment before it pounced again—but Tansy jumped into of its line of sight, her bright tail distracting the beast. As its attention fell on my familiar instead, my panic spiked for an entirely different reason.

"Hey!" I reached into my pocket and flung a handful of sage into the air, casting another levitation spell to push the herbs towards the creature. The beast staggered back, letting out an ear-splitting roar, while Tansy trembled on the ground.

Then, in a blink, the creature vanished. Sage showered the clearing, and I slumped against the nearest tree trunk. That was a close call. If I hadn't had the sceptre, those claws would have ended me. Like Rachel, who'd probably had no idea of what to expect.

Especially if someone had ordered her to summon the creature without telling her the risks. *This time I've got you, Tiffany.*

Tansy ran over to me, tail twitching. "Get us out of here. Before it comes back."

I pushed away from the tree. "I'm starting to see why the wildlife has been avoiding the forest."

I didn't blame them, given the overwhelming presence of a beast that scared the living daylights out of any creature that crossed its path. Including me. With Tansy clinging to my arm, I ran out of the clearing and didn't stop until I'd left the forest behind.

Outside, I found Ramsey leading a team of officers up the road. He came to an abrupt halt when he saw me. "What—Robin, why are you covered in leaves?"

"I just saw the monster. It ran off."

He groaned. "I should have known."

"I was right though." I bent double to catch my breath. "It's a beast from the afterworld, and I think Rachel summoned it right there in the clearing. The pentagram appeared when I cast a detection charm."

"The afterworld?" he repeated. "What manner of creature is it?"

"Like a giant wolf-bear," I said. "It's strong enough to throw off a spell I cast using my sceptre."

His eyes widened. "How is that possible?"

"Because necromancy breaks the usual rules of magic. I don't know if Rachel was aware of what she was doing, but I'm certain she wasn't acting alone."

His mouth parted. "If she summoned the creature before she died, then who is controlling the beast now?"

"Nobody," I replied. "Or whoever told Rachel to summon it in the first place."

His gaze went to the Henbane Coven's headquarters. "If there isn't any proof, then we'll have a repeat of the last incident."

"I know." The incident in question had been when I'd tried to catch her in the act of summoning Grandma's ghost, which really ought to have been a clue as to the kind of magic she dabbled in. Though there was a leap from summoning a ghost to setting that monster loose in the forest. "The evidence in the clearing counts as proof, given that there's a giant pentagram on top of the spot where Rachel vanished."

"That doesn't implicate Tiffany, unfortunately." Ramsey nodded to two members of his team. "Go and search the Henbane Coven's base for any evidence of them dabbling in illegal necromancy. Don't take no for an answer."

As they departed, both Mum and Jemima emerged from the Wildwood Coven's headquarters and made a beeline for us.

"I found it," I said before either of them could ask any questions. "I found the site of the summoning, and the monster... well, it kind of appeared on top of me when I revealed the pentagram."

Mum's face paled. "You saw the beast? Is it still there?"

"I scared it off," I told her. "It's lucky I had that sage, because even my sceptre didn't make an impact on that monster."

"Head Witch!" Isadora's voice came drifting down the road.

"We have company." Jemima's mouth thinned. "Unfortunately."

Sure enough, the other Head Witches came striding into view, Isadora leading the way with a scowl etched on her face. "What's this I hear about Mavis agreeing to talk to you and not us?"

"Someone summoned a hellish beast from the afterworld," I said to her. "It's running around the forest unchecked, so everything else will have to take a back seat until we can catch it. Does anyone here have knowledge of necromancy?"

Isadora's mouth fell open. "Did you just accuse me of practising illegal magic?"

"We need people with *knowledge* of necromancy, not

practical experience." Jemima stepped in. "That said, if you're all volunteering to help us out, then the support will be more than welcome."

Isadora drew herself upright. "I will do no such thing."

"Anyone else?" I turned towards Acacia. "Did the Seeing Stone warn you of this? Is that what it showed you?"

Mum shot me a warning look, but she didn't reprimand me for breaking etiquette.

"When I looked into the Stone, I saw the forest," Acacia said begrudgingly. "There was a person there… a young woman."

"Rachel?"

She didn't need to answer. The Stone had shown her the perpetrator, but she'd chosen not to share that information with anyone else.

"Rachel summoned that creature?" asked Isadora. "The first victim?"

"I suspect her coven leader put her up to it," I said. "Without warning her of the potential consequences. Mavis, I assume, inadvertently strayed too close to its hiding place. She didn't know it was hiding in the afterworld nearby."

"What did it look like?" one of Isadora's fellow coven members asked. "I'm not an expert, but I've a friend who knows a Reaper, and I might be able to identify the creature from the description."

"A cross between a bear and a wolf," I said. "With really big claws. Anyone know what that is?"

"A Ghast," the witch said in a soft voice. "Nasty creatures. Even a Reaper would have trouble controlling a Ghast."

"How did you find out it was a spirit?" Acacia asked me. "Have you been dabbling in necromancy yourself?"

Nice try. "My grandmother is a ghost. I worked it out."

"The former Head Witch?" Isadora asked. "What—?"

"Questions later," Jemima interjected. "Now we're all here, I think the collective strength of four Head Witches ought to be sufficient to deal with the creature."

"You're not volunteering us for this," Acacia protested. "I won't do it."

"You were happy to walk into the forest when you thought it was a regular beast, weren't you?" I couldn't resist taking a swipe at her. She more than deserved it after the way she'd acted so far. "I temporarily drove the creature away, but it'll be back, and we need to be ready."

"You drove it off?" Isadora asked. "How?"

"Sage repels the dead." I knew that much. "It jumped into the afterworld, but that doesn't mean it's gone."

My grandmother often vanished for hours at a time whenever she got into one of her sulks, but she was never far off. She also wouldn't be happy I'd told the others she'd stuck around, but it was her own fault for being so secretive in the first place.

"No, we'd need a permanent banishing spell," said Jemima. "Hmm. A spell to banish a ghost *might* work if we combined our strengths."

"There's one in that textbook." Leaving the other Head Witches to argue, I ran back to the witches' headquarters and made for my office. "Chloe, I need the herbs for a summoning spell."

"You—" She dropped the textbook, which she'd been engrossed in. "You're summoning it?"

"I might not even need herbs, with the sceptre," I

allowed. "Banishing it though… is there a spell to banish a spirit in there?"

"Yes." She began frantically flipping through the pages. "You think it'd work on a creature of that strength?"

"Maybe not with me alone, but the other Head Witches have generously volunteered to help. Or Mum and Jemima are working on convincing them, anyway."

Since I'd used a summoning spell fairly recently to summon Grandma's ghost, I didn't need to look that one up—and now I had the sceptre, I didn't need any props.

"Here." Chloe showed me the right page of the book. "A spell for banishing the dead. It's easier to cast the spell if you first set up a perimeter of sage to keep the target from running away."

"Good call." I went to the cabinet at the back of the office. "I'll get all the sage we have in stock."

Chloe helped me carry the sage outside, to where the other three Head Witches remained locked into an argument. The other council members both local and otherwise looked on, while Ramsey had joined his officers outside the Henbane Coven's base.

I cleared my throat to get the other Head Witches' attention. "I take it all of you know how to cast a summoning spell?"

"What do you take us for?" Acacia spluttered. "We're not *summoning* that creature."

"It's that or wait for it to find us first," I said. "I have the instructions on how to banish a ghost, but we'll need to put sage down to keep it contained."

"You are out of your mind," Acacia said faintly. "Where do you propose we summon this creature? Lives would be endangered."

"Not if we picked an enclosed space." Like, say, the garden of the person who'd originally summoned it. I approached Ramsey and the other officers, hearing Tiffany Henbane's voice coming from the doorway to the Henbane Coven's base.

"This is unjust!" she shrieked. "You're blaming me for crimes I never committed instead of investigating the guilty party. A shifter did this, mark my words."

"It's over, Tiffany," I said. "We know what you did."

She fixed her gaze on me. "I have no idea what you're talking about."

"I saw the pentagram in the forest on the spot where Rachel died," I said. "Or where the creature you asked her to summon slaughtered her on the spot. I'm sure if the police search your headquarters extensively, they'll find evidence of how she learned to cast that spell."

"This won't stand!" Tiffany yelled. "Rachel deserves better than to be slandered after her death."

"You as good as killed her when you set Rachel up to take the fall," I said. "And you've done nothing but try to derail the investigation into her death from the start."

Everything had been calculated. Accusing shifters, calling the press, distracting the officers in the forest... I couldn't believe I hadn't seen the truth sooner.

"Step aside," Ramsey commanded. "My officers intend to search your headquarters."

"*She* shouldn't be allowed in." She pointed at me, but the officers ignored her protests. Collectively, they drove her backwards into the lobby. I followed the police, and the other witches swarmed through the doors behind me. Even Isadora and Acacia. They might not have been keen on my plan, but they weren't about to miss out on the action.

While the police began their search, I made for the automatic glass doors at the back leading out into the garden. Chloe went into efficient assistant mode to pass out handfuls of sage to everyone willing to help, and in seemingly no time at all, we'd laid down a circle around a section of the garden.

Tiffany stood in the background, flanked by two officers. "You can't do this! You can't summon a monster in my garden. It's illegal."

"Summoning a monster with the intent of banishing it from this realm is within the boundaries of the law," Jemima told her. "Without access to the skills of a Reaper, this is our only option."

I stood on the boundary of the circle of sage. "I think if we want this to work, then we should all cast the banishment spell at the same time. Everyone who wields a sceptre."

Somehow, Chloe and Mum had coaxed the other two Head Witches into joining us in the back garden, along with their fellow coven members. Since the police and Tiffany were also present, there wasn't anywhere else they could stand without missing out on the drama.

"This is foolish," Acacia whispered.

"No more so than walking into the forest carrying a handmade trap," I said pointedly. "Ready?"

I was far from ready myself, my nerves thrumming and my legs trembling as if the ground were unsteady beneath my feet. With shaking hands, I held up the sceptre. If it was potent enough to summon the dead without any props, then I really hoped it could banish them as easily.

Tiffany watched, her expression like that of a cornered predator, while I pictured that terrifying bear-wolf creature in my mind's eye and cast the summoning spell.

Darkness pooled in front of us, and the bear-wolf creature appeared in a flash of claws. The Ghast lunged forward—and recoiled from the line of sage blocking its path.

I raised my sceptre. "Now the banishment. On your marks—"

Flashes of light came from the others' sceptres, slamming into the creature one after another—but it remained upright.

"We need more of us!" Mum shouted from the house, beckoning other witches to follow her. "At the same time!"

The creature roared and took a swipe at the sage, but I stalled it with a freezing charm. "On three. One, two, *three.*"

This time, more than a dozen spells hit the beast at once. The Ghast reeled back, its huge body suspended in the air. Then shadows folded around the beast, swallowing it up, until no traces remained.

All was quiet. I wrenched my gaze away and was rewarded with the sight of Aunt Shannon gaping at the spot where the creature had vanished, rendered speechless for possibly the first time in her life. Next to her, Vanessa sank to the ground. She'd passed out cold.

"Tiffany Henbane." Ramsey stepped forwards. "You're under arrest."

I'd hoped to hear those words for a long time, and it was completely worth the wait.

16

Mavis was discharged from the hospital the following morning, just in time for the delayed meeting. She was among the first to enter the council meeting room, walking without so much as a limp. The magical healers at the hospital had done their jobs well. Helena sat on her witch's shoulder, croaking happily.

When the last council member took her seat, Mavis removed the Seeing Stone from her bag and placed it on the table. I didn't know what she'd said to Acacia to convince her to return it to her for a day, but it must have been convincing. Acacia herself sat next to Isadora. Their truce seemed to have lasted, though from what I gathered, they'd each spoken to Mavis individually the previous day after Tiffany had been hauled away by the police.

"This meeting was intended to be a summary of the week's topics and a chance for us to lay out a solid plan for the future," I began. "That said, I'm sure the rest of you have other matters on your minds. If any of you has any questions, now's the time to ask them."

"What of the rest of the Henbane Coven?" Isadora asked without preamble. "Should they not be punished as well, for colluding with Tiffany Henbane in necromancy and other illegal magic?"

"The police confiscated several books from their premises and made some arrests," I said. "They're planning to conduct extensive interviews of the other members, but based on Rachel's fate, it's safe to say that Tiffany didn't tell everyone the true dangers of the magic she was dabbling in."

However little I cared for Tiffany herself, it didn't seem fair to punish members of her coven who'd never signed up to help her research illegal magic. Some people chose to join a coven, but others were born into it. Like my family, for instance.

"Is she simply going to be jailed then?" Acacia asked. "Such a crime merits a more severe punishment, in my opinion."

"She'll be jailed for life. Is that not enough?"

The police had put her under the highest security possible, while the rest of her coven would be placed under close watch. Acacia, however, was no doubt thinking of the prisons staffed by the paranormal hunters, who were rumoured to be uncompromising. Tiffany might deserve such a fate, but the rest of us didn't need to deal with the hunters rampaging around town.

Besides, it was kind of hard for her to argue for stationing the paranormal hunters in town when the average hunter couldn't even *see* ghosts. Or monstrous beasts from the afterworld, either. I had an inkling she'd have to shelve those plans for a while.

"I'd say that's more than sufficient," Jemima said. "What matters is ensuring that this never happens again."

The rest of the meeting proceeded as planned, though the others' attitudes towards me seemed to have notably shifted since I'd helped bring down the creature Tiffany had set loose.

Even Aunt Shannon held a new wariness in her expression, while Vanessa had been doing her best to keep her distance from me. It made a change from their usual disdain, and their reactions confirmed that neither of them had been involved in the same illegal magic as the Henbanes had dabbled in.

Towards the end of the meeting, we had an unexpected visitor. When I was in the process of calling the meeting to a close, Grandma appeared in the doorway with a dramatic "Boo!"

Everyone jumped, while Grandma let out a cackle. *Has she been waiting all week to do that?*

"Head Witch." Mavis didn't look surprised at her arrival. "It's good to see you again."

The rest repeated the sentiment, some sounding rather more sincere than others.

"You should have told us the former Head Witch endured beyond her death," Isadora said accusingly to me. "We would have liked to speak to her sooner."

"She wants to be left alone in her retirement," I said. "Right, Grandma?"

"Exactly." Grandma drifted forwards, causing Vanessa to nearly fall out of her seat in an effort to avoid her. "I had to see if you were handling things appropriately. Since nothing is currently on fire, I assume you are."

I hid a smile. I wouldn't lie, it was nice to see her unleash her most aggravating tendencies against someone other than me for a change.

Isadora rose to her feet, her expression harried. "I think we've discussed everything on the agenda. Any further issues in Wildwood Heath can be left to the local Head Witch to handle."

A murmur of agreement passed along the table. They trusted me to handle it, did they? Wonders would never cease.

As the others began to rise to their feet, I waited for everyone else to leave first. Isadora and Acacia were first to depart along with their entourages, followed shortly by the rest of the council. Aunt Shannon and Vanessa were long gone, of course. That left Mavis—and the Seeing Stone.

"Wasn't Acacia supposed to have that next?" I asked.

"I convinced her to let me keep it a little longer," said Mavis. "As compensation for my narrow escape."

I fidgeted and glanced at the door. Outside, Mum inclined her head in a nod. "Ah, may I borrow the Stone for a moment before you leave?"

"Of course," she said. "Go ahead. I won't pry."

"I appreciate it." I sat in the chair nearest to the glowing green stone, my heart drumming in anticipation. I knew that the odds of being given direct answers on why the sceptre had chosen me as its wielder were slim, since the Stone only showed the future, not the past—yet I still hoped.

I reached out my hand and laid my palm against the Seeing Stone. Green light suffused my vision, blanking out the rest of the room.

When the light dimmed, trees surrounded me on all sides. Was this the Wildwood? It was definitely a forest, but the trees were blurred around me, as if I was moving fast. Flying, perhaps. Shadows flitted in and out of the trees.

A familiar darkness gathered on the path in front of me. I knew those shadows. I'd seen them before. Someone was using necromancy.

I tried to turn my head, but the vision held me in its grip. My sceptre glowed in my outstretched hand, and I spun around on the spot—

The forest vanished at once, and the meeting room came back into focus. Cold sweat rose to the surface of my skin when I released the Stone, my hand trembling a little.

"Are you okay?" Mavis asked.

I nodded shakily. "Do visions usually not make much sense?"

"That's the nature of seeing the future," Mavis said, not unkindly. "I'll be consulting the Stone myself when I return home. Then I'll have to give it to Acacia, I'm afraid."

All right. This wouldn't be my last chance to consult a Stone, I was sure.

"Thank you," I said to her. "For everything."

While she packed the Stone away, supervised by Helena, I spotted Mum talking to Jemima outside the room.

"I should go," Jemima was saying. "I'll see you at the next summit."

The others said their goodbyes and headed towards the exit, where their luggage awaited them. Acacia took off with her entourage, as did Jemima, but Isadora lingered behind.

"I will see you at the next gathering," she said to me. "I look forward to it."

"So do I," I lied. At least any trouble we ran into at our next meeting wouldn't be traced back to Wildwood Heath. I'd think twice before volunteering our town as a meeting spot in the future, that was for sure.

Once Isadora and her allies had taken flight, Mavis and her toad approached my mother and me. "I wanted to thank you again for the work of your healers in saving my life."

"They're good at their jobs." I smiled. "I'm glad you're okay. Will you be flying home?"

"Yes, I've been declared fit to fly," she answered. "Then I intend to take a long rest."

"Sounds like a plan."

I waved Mavis and her familiar off as they took flight along with their fellow coven members, their flock of broomsticks gliding upwards into the sky.

When they were out of sight, Mum turned to me. "You used the Seeing Stone. What did you see?"

"I'm not entirely sure yet," I said slowly, "but I was in a forest... maybe the Wildwood. And... and I'm almost certain someone in there was using necromancy."

"Tiffany?"

"I didn't see. She's not getting out of jail anytime soon, right?"

"Absolutely not," Mum said. "However... according to Ramsey, she has no valid experience to explain how she was able to give Rachel the instructions to summon that beast. I have no idea how she obtained those books either."

A shiver travelled down my spine. "I'm sure she'll be full of excuses and keen to blame someone else."

If someone else had taught her, though, Tiffany might not be alone in the threat she presented. To the coven... and to the Head Witches.

Was that why the sceptre had chosen me? I hadn't directly asked the Stone, but the thoughts had been foremost in my mind when I'd touched its surface, and it was supposed to be attuned to the thoughts of anyone who held it. I'd always figured the sceptre had thrown itself into my hands because it had figured I was the best shot at helping the coven through whatever lay ahead, but I didn't know that it could sense the future in the way the Stone did.

Daunting though it might be, what was a little necromancy compared to what I'd already had to deal with?

With our guests gone, I gave everyone in the coven the rest of the day off. Nobody had any focus to speak of, even Mum, and Tansy was delighted when I offered to take her into the Wildwood for a walk. Birdsong filled the trees, a sign that the forest was already returning to normal, and—wait, what were Clarice and Speck doing here?

I came to a halt on the forest path. "You're not supposed to be here."

As promised, they'd printed the interview based on our chat yesterday that morning, which I'd skimmed to make sure they'd kept their word. I should have guessed that wouldn't be enough for them.

"We heard you caught the person behind the recent attacks," Speck said. "Since you told us not to interview anyone else in your family, we hoped you might be willing to talk to us again."

At least they hadn't called Harvey. "It depends if you think your readership can handle learning about terrifying necromantic monsters from the afterworld."

Clarice stared at me. "Is that true? We heard rumours, but we kept our word…"

So they had. I almost wanted to give them a second interview for that reason alone. "Yes, it's true. Tiffany Henbane summoned a dangerous monster from the afterworld, and it took the collective efforts of me and all the other Head Witches in town to banish it before it could harm anyone else. If you want to print those words and attribute them to me, feel free."

Clarice hurried to get out a notepad to scribble down my words, while Speck turned on his recording equipment.

"Also," I added, "given that I was the one who got rid of the creature, I'd hold off on printing speculation about whether I'm fit for the position of Head Witch—or else I might not be around to deal with the next one."

Speck gulped. "Right. Of course."

Both of them jumped violently when the bushes rustled. I hid a grin, especially when I saw Tansy scuffling around underneath, making the leaves sway.

Footsteps crunched, and Ramsey and several other officers walked into view from the other end of the woodland path.

"Oh… it's the police," said Clarice faintly. "Good. We'll be on our way."

"Are they giving you trouble?" Ramsey called to me. "Should I escort them out of town?"

"No, they can see themselves out." I gave both of them a pointed stare until they fled into the forest, while Tansy emerged from the bushes, snickering to herself. "What are you doing in here?"

"Looking for those reporters, for one thing," he said. "What did you say to them?"

"I gave them a short statement. That's all they're getting from me."

"Good," said Ramsey. "There's no traces of the creature left. It's gone."

"Just what I like to hear." Above the trees, I saw the last of the witches' broomsticks vanish into the sky. "Anything else?"

Ramsey paused for a long moment. "You're not so bad at being Head Witch."

"Wow. A compliment." I kept my tone light, teasing, while Tansy scaled a nearby tree and called mockingly to a group of pigeons. "Thanks."

"I'll see you later," he said. "Ah—I have the evening off. Want to watch a movie?"

"You mean do I want to watch you sleep through a movie? Sure."

I had a whole afternoon ahead of me, and I intended to make the most of it. First, I'd drop by and visit my dad. Then I needed to tell Rowan and Piper everything. Harvey too. I was sure he'd be happy to postpone our next date so I could spend some quality time with my brother. If the past couple of weeks had taught me anything, it was to treasure the moments when we weren't at one another's throats.

Oh, and that I could always count on Tansy's instincts to be on the mark. She ran through the treetops overhead, while the birds' cries filled the background in a riot of noise. The Wildwood was well and truly back.

ABOUT THE AUTHOR

Elle Adams lives in the middle of England, where she spends most of her time reading an ever-growing mountain of books, planning her next adventure, or writing. Elle's books are humorous mysteries with a paranormal twist, packed with magical mayhem.

She also writes urban and contemporary fantasy novels as Emma L. Adams.

Visit http://www.elleadamsauthor.com/ to find out more about Elle's books.

9 781915 250407